"You picked the wrong house to freeload in."

Archer felt grim satisfaction in the woman's startled jump as she spun around to face him after he spoke.

Holy hell. He knew this woman. A shaft of white-hot misery speared his insides and his voice cracked with surprise as he managed to murmur her name, though in truth it was a miracle his voice worked at all, his shock was so great.

As he stared at the face that haunted his dreams, he couldn't help but drink in her appearance, even if he'd never admit to anyone—least of all her—that losing her had been as painful as tearing off a limb and tossing it down the garbage disposal.

"Marissa." He recovered, ashamed at his gut reaction and the sudden leap in his heartbeat, and demanded, "What the hell are you doing here?"

Dear Reader,

There is something to be said for the allure of rekindling a lost love. We all have someone in our past that we can't help but wonder "what if?" Sometimes the road not taken is a benefit to both parties as the relationship was bound to fizzle or implode. Other times, it's hard to ignore that section of the heart that still yearns for the one who got away because we wonder, deep down, if they might've been The One.

For Marissa Vasquez and Archer Brant, circumstance throws them together and the threat of danger keeps them close, but it's love that ultimately binds them. Writing their story was a roller coaster of ups and downs as they struggled against their need for one another, and the reward was that much sweeter when they conquered their challenges.

This is the last story in the HOME IN EMMETT'S MILL miniseries. It's been a wonderful journey. I hope you enjoy this story of redemption and second chances.

Hearing from readers is one of my greatest joys (aside from really good chocolate) so don't be shy. Feel free to drop me a line at my Web site, www.kimberlyvanmeter.com, or through snail mail at P.O. Box 2210, Oakdale, CA 95361.

Happy reading,

Kimberly Van Meter

Trusting the Bodyguard

Kimberly Van Meter

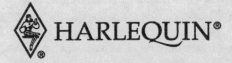

HARLEQUIN®

TORONTO • NEW YORK • LONDON
AMSTERDAM • PARIS • SYDNEY • HAMBURG
STOCKHOLM • ATHENS • TOKYO • MILAN • MADRID
PRAGUE • WARSAW • BUDAPEST • AUCKLAND

Recycling programs
for this product may
not exist in your area.

ISBN-13: 978-0-373-71627-2

TRUSTING THE BODYGUARD

ABOUT THE AUTHOR

An avid reader since before she can remember, Kimberly Van Meter started her writing career at the age of sixteen when she finished her first novel, typing late nights and early mornings on her mother's portable typewriter. Although that first novel was nothing short of literary mud, with each successive piece of work her writing improved, to the point of reaching that coveted published status.

Kimberly, now a journalist, and her husband and three kids make their home in Oakdale, California. She enjoys writing, reading, photography and drinking hot chocolate by the windowsill when it rains.

Books by Kimberly Van Meter

HARLEQUIN SUPERROMANCE
1391—THE TRUTH ABOUT FAMILY
1433—FATHER MATERIAL*
1469—RETURN TO EMMETT'S MILL*
1485—A KISS TO REMEMBER
1513—AN IMPERFECT MATCH*
1577—KIDS ON THE DOORSTEP*
1600—A MAN WORTH LOVING*

*Home in Emmett's Mill

To those who've had the good fortune to reconnect with their heart's desire and equally to those who've found contentment in allowing the past to remain in memory.
Everything happens as it should.

CHAPTER ONE

ARCHER BRANT SLIPPED his key in the lock of his front door, still surly over the forced convalescence dictated by the Bureau doc. The three-hour drive from San Francisco had at least leached most of his anger so that he didn't feel the need to punch something any longer. He gritted his teeth against the pulsing ache in his busted-up shoulder and thoughts of a beer with a Vicodin chaser crossed his mind, but the moment he stepped over the threshold of his cabin, the hairs on the back of his neck stiffened with a sense that something wasn't right.

Quietly pocketing his keys, he moved to the scarred oak cabinet where he kept his spare Glock and retrieved it slowly from the drawer. Once the comforting weight of the gun was in his hand, he moved through the bottom floor of his house in a security sweep. Finding nothing, he made his way up the stairs.

His ears pricked at an odd, unfamiliar sound coming from his bedroom.

Creeping along the wall, he pushed open the door to his bedroom and slid inside. Someone was in his bathroom. The air still held the balmy, damp moisture left over from a hot shower. He caught the sound of soft singing, slightly off tune and he wondered what kind of idiot broke into a stranger's house to make use of the soap and shampoo as if it was a friggin Holiday Inn yet bypassed the valuables like the flat-screen plasma television mounted on the wall or the accompanying high-end Bose stereo system. He curled his lip. Whoever was in there was murdering a classic Journey song, and that was near enough to a crime in his book to warrant shooting first and asking questions later. Since he was supposed to be convalescing, he ignored his itchy trigger finger and his protesting ear drums and just prepared to oust his uninvited houseguest with a little force.

He moved into position along the wall, gaining an excellent vantage point, and his disposition brightened at the thought of scaring the life out of the trespasser. But as a figure moved into view of the mirror, Archer blinked and frowned with surprise. He'd been expecting a punk pimply-faced kid or perhaps a homeless man but he was damn sure not expecting to see dark hair cascading down a petite backside that was nearly engulfed in his white terry cloth robe. Strong, slim legs, rounded calves and pretty ankles met his gaze as he assessed his trespasser. A woman. A shapely woman, he noted with faint appreciation for the rounded swell of hips hidden beneath the robe, and even as his hormones pumped a healthy dose of testosterone into his veins, he looked for evidence of a partner. A beautiful woman provided great distraction for the thug that's about to cave in your cranium from the back. That's not how he was going to clock out of this world.

But his quick check revealed nothing, not even a bag of belongings. Then on the bed he saw something that narrowed his stare and made him swear under his breath.

A baby bottle. Leaking something wet and pale onto his five-hundred-dollar duvet. "This just ain't my day," he muttered, tucking his gun into his waistband. Of all the places this wayward chick could've stopped, why'd it have to be his? He wasn't in the mood to play host no matter what her hard luck story was. He pinched the bridge of his nose and exhaled a short breath before stepping into view, ready to get this over with. "You picked the wrong house to freeload in," he announced, taking grim satisfaction in the woman's startled jump as she spun around to face him.

But holy hell, the air in his lungs evaporated and it felt as though his heart had squeezed to a stuttering stop. He knew this woman. A shaft of white-hot misery speared his insides and his voice cracked with surprise as he managed to murmur her name, though in truth it was a miracle his voice worked at all, his shock was so great. As he stared at the face that haunted his dreams and took center stage in his most private thoughts, he couldn't help but drink in her appearance, even if he'd never admit to anyone—least of all her—that losing her had been as painful as shoving a limb into a garbage grinder. And just as permanent.

"Marissa." He recovered, ashamed at his gut reaction and the sudden leap in his heartbeat, to demand, "What the hell are you doing here?"

MARISSA VASQUEZ'S PALMS found and then clutched the marble countertop she was leaning against. She'd rehearsed a possible explanation while in the shower but now that Archer was standing before her, looking fierce and stony, her well-rehearsed speech fled along with the strength in her knees. Suddenly, she was well aware of her near nakedness, her busted lip and the sheer improbability that Archer would find it in his heart to help her at all.

And who could blame him, she thought bitterly. The last time she saw him she was breaking off their engagement. The shock in his eyes was slowly replaced by something cold and hard and she felt her chances dwindling to next to nothing. But desperation was a powerful motivator and she had nowhere else to turn.

"I can explain," she said nervously as she tried to hold on to a shred of dignity to get her through this.

She ducked down and scooped her niece, Jenna, from the floor where she'd been hidden from view and held her close for strength. The toddler twisted in her arms to stare at Archer, her finger popping in her mouth as she watched him with open curiosity.

"Please do." Archer's gaze skipped for a brief moment to the baby before returning to her, and she realized she wasn't sure where to start. He settled against the wall in a totally casual pose that belied the tense set of his jaw. She faltered and her throat closed against the rush of fear and grief that threatened to reduce her to a puddle of pathetic tears if she didn't just start somewhere.

"Clock's tickin'," he said with a cruelly arched brow that emphasized just how short his patience with her was at the moment.

She adjusted Jenna on her hip while trying to keep the too large robe from gaping open. "Well, I—I needed—no, thought, that, um, well, it's c-complicated," she stammered. Tears welled in her eyes but she blinked them back. Archer was not going to help her. She swallowed convulsively when the image of her dead sister flashed in her mind and the phantom smell of her sister's blood filled her nostrils. He was her one and only hope. And judging by the cool assessing stare she was getting, that hope had been grossly misplaced. The urge to collapse in a heap and bawl was too strong for words but she couldn't in front of Archer. Not like this. She lifted her chin and though her mouth trembled, she managed to say, "We'll be out of your hair soon. I just needed a place to get cleaned up."

"Get to the explaining part, Marissa," he growled, his expression unreadable. When her tongue seemed paralyzed, he said mockingly, "What happened to the biotech scientist who'd had her heart set on a tidy little condo in Los Gatos and didn't want or need complications in her life?" She recovered sufficiently to return an angry stare for throwing her last words to him in her face when she was clearly at a disadvantage. But before she could rebound with a cutting comment of her own, he pushed off the wall and walked toward her, sending her pulse into an epileptic fit so that she had to breathe a little deeper to keep from visibly trembling. "Not interested in sharing details? How about this? Skip to the good parts. Just tell me how it is that you're in my bathroom with a busted-up face and a baby. I'm a pretty sharp guy but I'm going to need you to connect the dots on this one."

Her lip throbbed. She touched the swollen flesh with the tip of her tongue and winced with the sharp pain. It was hard to forget that she looked like hell but now was not the time for vanity. Besides, even if she had showed up looking like a supermodel, it was unlikely Archer would've been swayed. She waved him away, defeat and fear making her reckless.

"Forget it. I thought… Never mind. It doesn't matter. We'll be out of here in a few minutes."

Something flicked across his expression—grudging concern?—and it was that flash that made her pause when he said her name again.

"What's going on?" he asked. "And who's the kid? Yours?"

She thought of lying. But she couldn't, not with Archer staring at her like he was. "I'm in trouble," she said in a small voice.

"That's apparent," he retorted then gestured at Jenna. "And the kid?"

"My sister's."

"Mercedes," he acknowledged softly, his sharp gaze narrowing in thought. "So where is that wild sister of yours, then?"

"Dead." Her voice choked on the word. "She's dead."

He swore and looked away. A long time ago when Marissa had thought she was going to marry Archer, she'd filled him in on her family life that started with a single mom and an unruly sister who was more trouble than a pack of brothers, growing up on the bad side of Oakland. He must've remembered what she'd told him about Mercedes. He didn't seem surprised. "Who's the father?" he asked finally.

Marissa hesitated, unsure. Should she tell Archer the whole truth of what was going on? As she hedged, she realized her mistake. Archer, even after all this time, could still read her as easily as the Sunday paper and as he waited she knew it was pointless to lie. "His name is Ruben Ortiz. He runs the Oaktown Boyz gang on the East Side. Mercedes met him while she was cocktailing at a new club called Porters."

"Let me guess, this Ruben character owns the club," Archer surmised.

She nodded. "And when he saw Mercedes…he had to have her. I told her he was bad news but she didn't listen. All she saw was the fancy cars, the jewelry and the parties," she said bitterly, looking away before the shine in her eyes betrayed her grief. Somehow her life had been turned into an episode from a crime drama and she had no control over how it ended. Her biggest fear was that her end would be similar to her sister's and the thought chilled her blood. "And she changed. Though, at the end, it seemed, maybe, she'd gone back to the way she was before. But it was too late."

Archer took everything in and seemed to digest the information, yet didn't seem overly interested in too many details. Not that she blamed him particularly. If she weren't knee-deep in the mess herself, she'd have steered clear, as well.

"Get dressed and come downstairs. Something tells me I'm going to need a beer to hear the rest of this story."

A pang of sadness, different from the grief she lived with now, pierced her chest and she had to wonder if coming to Archer had been the wisest decision. It was apparent water was not under the bridge. Archer still harbored some bitter feelings over their breakup even though it'd been nearly three years since that sunny day on the park bench outside her lab. She made quick work of dragging on her dirty clothes, grimacing at the stale feeling and the lingering smell of cigar smoke that clung to the fabric. She looked longingly at Archer's closet and wished she could grab a T-shirt to slip on instead but she'd lost the right to rummage through his things with such familiarity, and so after putting a clean diaper on the baby and grabbing her bottle, she and Jenna went downstairs to face a man who was their only hope for survival.

ARCHER'S THOUGHTS WERE in a twisted mess. Thank God for training to fall back on when faced with a crisis. He could thank the Corps for the foundation and the Bureau for the fine-tuning. Marissa was in his house. With a baby, no less.

At first, his gut plummeted when he thought the kid might be hers. There was no sense in lying, he'd been relieved when she admitted the baby was her older sister's. But the relief that followed filled him with misgivings.

He shouldn't care who or what Marissa had been up to since the day she cracked his heart in two and handed it to him impaled on a steak knife. As far as he was concerned she could get run down by a runaway taxicab and he wouldn't shed a tear.

So if that was the case, why did seeing her so visibly scared and physically roughed up fill him with such rage that he wanted to shoot something? Because it wouldn't be right to walk away when she was clearly desperate. So they've got history. So what? That part of him was dead and long past capable of resurrection.

She came down the stairs and, even though he tried hard not to notice, he couldn't help but remember each gentle curve of her body and the lush breasts that seemed to fill his palm as perfectly as if they were made just for him. He deliberately cut away his stare, affecting a casual pose as he cracked open his beer and took a deep slug of the microbrew.

She took a seat on the sofa, hugging the baby to her chest. The child yawned loudly and settled against Marissa. He wondered what kind of life the kid had been living with Mercedes for a mother. From what he remembered, Mercedes Vasquez had been the exotic type, with tastes that ran to the extreme, which explained the hookup with a known gangster.

But that didn't explain why Marissa was the one sitting in front of him looking as though she'd taken a nasty crack across the face, holding a baby that didn't belong to her.

"The cabin is just as I remembered it," Marissa started, glancing away, as if she couldn't stand to look him in the eye. "Except the yard. I don't re-member the weeds last time I was here."

"I'm not much of a gardener." He placed his beer on the granite-topped coffee table with deliberate slowness, and then met her gaze. "What's going on, Marissa? Why are you in trouble?"

She swallowed. "Ruben killed my sister."

"Did you witness the crime?"

"No, but I know he did it."

"How so?"

Her mouth tightened but her eyes watered. "Be-cause he swore he would kill her if she tried to keep Jenna from him. She'd just gotten a restraining order against him the day before I found her with a bullet in the back of her head."

"You found your sister's body?"

Her bottom lip trembled. "Yes. In her apartment."

Sympathy softened his voice. "I'm sorry. That's rough. What happened next?"

She drew a deep breath. "I called 911. They came and took Mercedes away and I called Ruben."

"Why?"

"Because I needed him to think that I didn't suspect him so I could get to Jenna. I knew he had her. There was no sign of Jenna in the apartment and her diaper bag was gone."

"So you went to Ruben's house?"

"More like a compound than a house," she nearly spat, contempt pinching her supple mouth into a hard line. "Ruben lives like a king in the Oakland Hills. He may run East Side but he sure as hell doesn't live there. I went to get Jenna. Even if he hadn't killed Mercedes, he isn't fit to raise a child."

"Wouldn't that be for the courts to decide?" he asked, his mind quickly putting together the scenario and not liking the way it ended. She glared and tightened her arms around the baby protectively. He shrugged. "If he's as bad as you say…"

"He is and worse."

He let that slide for the moment. "Something tells me he didn't just hand you his daughter."

"No."

"Is that how you got the busted lip?"

She glanced away, self-conscious. "Not exactly."

"How exactly?"

"One of Ruben's cousins caught me as I was sneaking out of the nursery. He got in a lucky punch."

"How'd you manage to get away?" His frown deepened. "If this guy is as dangerous as you say he is, it's likely his guards are armed. Am I right?"

She drew a shuddering breath and nodded but she didn't elaborate.

"Marissa…"

A red stain crept up her neck, spilling onto her cheeks and she refused to look at him. Something went down at that compound that she doesn't want to share, he mused silently, concern and his innate need to know warring with the instinct to give her some money and send her on her way. He didn't know this Ruben character but he was familiar with the Oaktown Boyz gang—a vicious street gang with ties to the Colombian drug trade, not a bunch of posers trying to look cool. They were the real deal and very dangerous.

"Archer…I'm exhausted," she said simply and looked to him to answer her unspoken plea. She must've known he wouldn't refuse her shelter, if not his protection, and she was right. He wasn't about to kick a defenseless woman and child out on the streets when they had nowhere to go, but she had to know also that he would do things his way, not hers.

"You can take the spare bedroom," he said, "but tomorrow I want the whole story, Marissa, not the *Reader's Digest* version or else I place a phone call and the choice is taken out of your hands."

She hesitated, clearly displeased with the terms of his hospitality but sheer fatigue won out over her stubborn nature and for that he was secretly relieved. Marissa had never been one to capitulate easily, her pride being nearly as strong as her backbone. It'd been one of the things he'd loved about her—but also what had torn them apart. She gathered the baby close and headed for the stairs. As she reached the landing, she offered a stiff, yet grateful "Thank you" and then made her way up to her bedroom.

CHAPTER TWO

MARISSA ROSE EARLY just as she always did before her life took a catastrophic turn for the worse. While the baby still slept, Marissa went into the adjoining bathroom and quickly scrubbed her face and ran her finger over her teeth to freshen up as best as she could.

Her hair, wavy and loose, looked untamed and messy but there was little she could do about that seeing as she'd busted out of Ruben's place with nothing more than the baby's diaper bag and a healthy dose of insanity and rage to keep her going. She'd been too afraid to pack anything for fear of Ruben getting suspicious. And she certainly couldn't go back to her condo because that's the first place Ruben would've sent his thugs looking for her. So, she had nothing in the way of toiletries and the thought of wearing the same pair of underwear for the next couple of days was too gross to contemplate. She'd have to go shopping. Although, if memory served, Emmett's Mill wasn't exactly a bustling metropolis; she'd be hard-pressed to find much more than the basics at the handful of small boutique-style shops on the main street.

She wandered to the window and peered through the glass to the breaking dawn. The sun crested the horizon in a warm blaze, casting gentle rays of light along the tops of bull and sugar pine trees that dotted the mountainside of the Sierra National Forest, creating an idyllic scene if she were of a mind to appreciate it. But right now her thoughts were crowded with details that she'd rather forget.

White Berber carpeting drenched in a pool of red.

Marissa squeezed her eyes shut for a heartbeat.

Dull, lifeless brown eyes staring at nothing.

A strangled sob erupted from her throat even as she tried to muffle the sound with her knuckles. Dead. Her sister was *dead.* Damn it, Mercedes.

She wiped at the wet trails leaking from the corners of her eyes and focused on the glistening patches of snow that had clung to the ground in stubborn spots, defying the warmth of the spring-time sun. It wouldn't be long before they completely melted and disappeared. Wiping the last of the moisture from her cheeks, she drew a deep breath and tried to pull what she needed from what little well of strength she had left. Archer was already awake—she'd heard his footfalls on the stairs—and he'd soon want to return to their previous topic of conversation. Whether she wanted to or not.

She checked Jenna, found her to be sleeping still, and then quietly went downstairs.

She was not surprised to see Archer in the kitchen, fully dressed and ready for anything, at 6:00 a.m. That had been one of the things they had in common. They both were ridiculously early risers. She ignored the faint sadness at the memory and gestured toward the coffeepot. "May I?"

"Help yourself," he said, taking a sip from his own steaming mug as he looked out the wide kitchen window.

It was entirely too strange to be here with Archer under these circumstances when the last time they'd enjoyed the view from the kitchen, they'd spent the morning making love in various and inventive ways. Three years was a long time to go without… She felt heat creeping into her cheeks and she moved away before Archer could read her expression and give her one of his famous narrowed stares that would only make her blush harder. There were things she certainly did not feel like sharing at the moment and that included the details of her sex life. Up until two days ago, Archer had been the last person she'd been intimate with. She liked to tell herself that she just hadn't found anyone compatible in that way, but you have to date to get to that next level and Marissa had buried herself in work, precluding a social life. "How have you been?" she asked, unable to stomach the silence between them. "You look good."

He spared her a glance then returned his stare to the view, and she huffed a short breath. "I see. As soon as the baby is awake we'll be on our way. Thanks for the bed and the pleasant company."

The last part was probably in bad form seeing as she was the one who'd invaded his space without warning, but she was stung by his open rejection and her verbal filters weren't functioning quite yet. She'd forgotten how rigid he could be, but it was all coming back to her in a rush of disappointment. When Archer chose to be obstinate, he took it to an art form.

"Marissa, we have to finish our talk from last night, remember?"

She stopped and turned. "The way I see it, we are finished."

"Well, we're not," he said, stalking past her to the living room, expecting her to follow. She was half-tempted to charge right up the stairs just to give him the message that she didn't take orders from him and never would, but she didn't put it past him to throw her over his shoulder and toss her to the sofa if she tried, so she grudgingly followed. He took a seat in an oversize recliner that would've swallowed her but seemed to fit his frame perfectly and waited for her to sit down across from him. She gave him a cold look but sat without getting too comfortable. The tension between them was heavy enough to choke the oxygen from her lungs. "Baby still asleep?" he asked, throwing her off with his concern.

"Yes. She seems to take after her mom and likes to sleep in," she said, covering her surprise with a bracing sip of her coffee. "What do you want to talk about?"

"I need to know everything that happened the night you took Jenna. Don't spare any details."

"Why?" she asked, hating to even think about that night and the ramifications. "It's not necessary."

"Let me be the judge of that. If you want my help, you're going to be honest with me. I don't want to be sucker punched by something later."

It was a fair request. If only the details didn't make her quake with equal parts revulsion and fear. She bit her lower lip, wondering how this became her life. Three days ago her biggest concern was whether her drug trial was going to be successful; now she was terrified of ending up like her sister and Jenna landing back in her father's arms. Tears filled her eyes before she could stop them. She looked away until she could blink them back.

"I'm sorry," she said, her voice trembling in spite of her attempt to keep it level and calm. "I wasn't thinking. I just came here because I knew that no one in Ruben's circle would know about you or this place and I figured we'd be safe here but I shouldn't have dragged you into this. It's not fair to you and I'm so sorry."

"You can always count on me, Marissa," he said roughly, as if it cost him to admit that. "I know you wouldn't have come if you didn't think it was your last option but I have to know everything."

She closed her eyes, blocking out the images that were stuck there. Sordid, disgusting and debasing images jumped to the forefront and she had to choke back a groan.

"What happened, Marissa?"

She looked away. "If I tell you, you have to promise me you won't tell anyone else." His pause made her jerk to face him and her heart squeezed painfully as she assessed him openly. His answer made the difference whether she shared or not. "Are you saying you can't keep this between us?"

"Depends on what you tell me," he answered, his tone deceptively mild, yet the burn in his eyes told another story. "I'm a federal agent. I can't make the rules up as I go along."

Contempt colored her voice. "Bullshit, that's exactly what you do in that secret branch you work for. Eyes Only, plausible deniability… I'm not an idiot, Archer."

"You just kidnapped the daughter of a known drug lord," he countered, making her see red. It wasn't as though she had a choice.

"He killed my sister! How could I leave Jenna with him?" Tears filled her eyes again but this time they were caused by rage, not fear or pain. "He's a bastard who destroys lives. I couldn't let her grow up with him. Not after what he did to her mother."

Her outburst didn't seem to sway him either way. She wiped at the moisture, irritation at his cold nature washing over her. She'd forgotten about that part of his personality, as well. Hell, had she remembered anything about him that was accurate? "You don't know what it's been like since Ruben came into our lives. It's been hell."

She didn't want to tell Archer that she'd often felt Ruben's gaze on her, sliding up and down her body, blatantly resting on her breasts as if it were his right to do so, not even hiding his perusal from the eyes of her sister. Mercedes had tried not to show that it bothered her, hurt her even, but toward the end, it had become unbearable. Marissa's only escape had been work, the one place Ruben was not allowed access. The day Mercedes had decided to end the relationship, Marissa had nearly cried with joy. Looking back, she realized what fools they'd been to think it would be that easy.

"Did he hurt you?" he asked, then clarified. "Physically."

She resisted the urge to touch her bruised face. Technically, Ruben hadn't lifted a finger. He had enough people around to do his dirty work. Upstairs the baby whimpered and she shot up. "Jenna's awake. I have to go get her."

Without waiting for his permission, she flew up the stairs and cuddled Jenna's sweet, pudgy body against her own. "Good morning, *mija,*" she whispered against her niece's crown and offered a word of gratitude to St. Jude, the patron saint of lost causes, then prepared to return downstairs to the man who would settle for nothing but the truth.

The problem was, the truth was something he was likely to wish he didn't know. God knows, she wished she could forget.

ARCHER DELIBERATELY KEPT his attention far from Marissa's retreating backside as she hurried to get the baby. At one time, he'd thought their babies would be the ones she'd be tending but that hadn't worked out so well. He gulped the rest of his coffee and then stood, unable to sit still any longer. His nerves were drawn tight and he was getting that edge that he always did at the start of an assignment. All that was missing was the actual assignment. And if the doc were to be believed...he was a long way from getting an assignment anytime soon. He swore and absently rubbed at his injury.

"What's wrong with your shoulder?"

Marissa's voice at his back made him turn to face her. He waved away the concern he saw there, uncomfortable with the way it made him want it. "It's nothing," he said brusquely. He gestured toward the baby. "Does she need anything?"

She eyed him hesitantly, as if doing an internal question-and-answer session to see how the conversation might turn out in real time, then nodded. "Diapers and milk."

"Milk I've got," he said. "Diapers I don't."

Her full, sensual mouth—he'd never quite forgotten how it felt sliding across his own—twisted in a wry grin. "Well, I'd have been surprised to hear otherwise. Is there a store close by I could go to? I need to pick up a few other things, too, before we take off."

He ignored the part where she mentioned leaving and grabbed a magnetic notepad from the refrigerator door. She was crazy if she thought he was going to let her leave when there was a murdering drug lord on her back. Plus there was the not-so-small detail that she'd kidnapped a toddler to deal with. It was best to keep her close for the time being. "What do you need? I'll get it for you."

"I don't need you to do that," she protested. "I have money and a car. I just need directions."

"Marissa...stop being stubborn. You need supplies. I will get them for you. End of story."

"Is this how it's going to be?" she demanded. "You giving orders like some drill sergeant? I didn't come here so you could boss me around. I'm perfectly capable of taking care of myself—"

"If that were the case you wouldn't have broken into my house with nothing more than the clothes on your back and the piss and vinegar in your blood," he cut in, ignoring the flash of wounded pride that followed. He couldn't afford to be moved by that beautiful face. It was bad enough that she had haunted his dreams and made him a miserable bastard during the day for the past three years. He sure as hell didn't need to let her get further under his skin. He grabbed his keys and pointed a finger at her. "Don't leave. I'll be back in an hour." He wasn't surprised when she didn't take kindly to his instruction.

"I don't appreciate being told what to do and when to do it. I'm not a child, nor your wife. I can come and go as I see fit."

True. But he wasn't going to see her get killed over this mess she'd gotten herself into. That was the last thing he needed on his conscience. He hardened his voice to drive the point home. "You're on the run with a kid that doesn't belong to you. All it will take is one phone call and your pretty little ass will be sitting in prison and that baby will return to her father."

Her eyes watered. "You would do that to me?" her whispered voice cut at him. "You would turn me in?"

"Yes."

He'd crushed her. He could see it in her face. He looked away so he wouldn't have to see it anymore. "It's not going to come to that. You'll stay because I'm the only one you can trust, Rissa," he said, his nickname for her flowing from his mouth too naturally for comfort. "Just stay put, will you?" he bit out before slamming the door behind him.

He used the drive to town to place a few phone

calls. He needed background information on this Ruben guy. With any luck the man had a record and an active warrant but even as he thought it, he knew his luck wouldn't be that good. Guys like Ruben slid in and out of bad situations on the power of their own slime and often came out the other side smelling like a rose and looking none the worse for their experience.

"I need a favor," he said, adjusting his Bluetooth device for a better position in his ear.

"Aren't you supposed to be resting or something like that?" Rico Harley said drily. "Heard Doc didn't give you the green light. Tough break. The downtime must be killing you."

Rico, a fellow special ops agent who was recruited by the FBI at the same time as Archer, was the kind of man who was wicked smart and just a little on the damaged side. Made him perfect for the kind of assignments they were given. Archer also knew that Rico wouldn't mind doing a little background for him. Rico liked to break the rules even more so than Archer.

"I need you to run a name."

"Dating again?" Rico returned indolently.

"Cut the crap. This is serious."

"What's the name?" Rico said, all business.

"Ruben Ortiz, rumor has it he runs Oaktown Boyz. Name ring any bells?"

"East Side Oakland Oaktown Boyz?"

"The very same."

"That's some sick shit. What you into?"

He hesitated then relented. Rico was solid. "Not me. A friend."

Rico's bark of laughter made him growl. "Now I know you're lying. You ain't got friends."

"Just run the damn name, funny boy."

"Why can't you do it? You've got clearance."

"Not right now I don't. If word gets out I was anywhere near the building Doc won't ever clear me. That sick SOB is just loving the fact that I'm out of commission."

"You might be right. For a doc, he's a sadistic asshole, ain't he?"

Rico's easy laughter cracked a reluctant grin from Archer. "So can you do me this favor? Or should I ask Jeremiah?"

"Good luck with that. Jeremiah went out on assignment last week."

Jeremiah was already out on assignment? Jealousy at his former team member getting the all-clear before him coupled with anger at himself for making such a stupid mistake drained the levity from his voice. "Fine. Call my cell when you get the info."

Rico didn't ask further questions, just agreed and the conversation was over. Men in general didn't chew the fat on the phone, but men in their profession found superfluous time spent on anything that could be traced was a liability.

Yeah, they were all that paranoid. Made them good at their jobs. Archer ignored the little voice in his head that was quick to point out that he was no longer the best, but the slaughtered body of Kandy Kane, aka Cynthia Harvey, was hard to forget. He was forced to wonder if the glory days were over. The thought, a chilling one, made him edgy and twitchy. Fact was, he loved his job the way some guys loved their wives. And his wife had just kicked him out of bed. That sucked hard. Deal with it, Brant. Just deal with it, he told himself sourly. He had a kid needing diapers and a former fiancée to keep safe. No sense in crying over what couldn't be fixed at the moment. Yeah…right.

CHAPTER THREE

MARISSA RAN A BRUSH through Jenna's thick hair, gently finger-combing the sweet baby curls that clung to her little head and hummed a mindless tune for the child's benefit. There was little else she could do at the moment but keep her safe and entertained until Archer returned with supplies.

She rolled her neck to relieve the tension bunching her shoulders up around her ears and groaned when a soft pop sounded. She was not the kind of person to sit idly, and doing just that was eating at her ability to hold on to her sanity. It was difficult to comprehend just how radically her life had changed within the space of two days. On the surface she missed the comfort of her routine—her early-morning run, a nonfat latte with whip cream and a quiet lunch spent under the trees in the park near the lab—but deep down there was a knot of grief that pulsed like an angry wound.

God, how she had loved her older sister but she wasn't going to lie…Mercedes had driven her crazy with her impetuous and often self-absorbed actions. And now…her life was unrecognizable because of Mercedes.

When Mercedes had told her she was pregnant, the air had left Marissa's lungs. Her sister's elated expression had given her no similar feeling. Inside, she'd felt a terrible sense of foreboding. Not for the child itself, for all children were gifts from God, but she'd known Ruben was the father and he made her skin crawl.

Jenna grinned and then squealed with delight when she latched on to the television remote. Marissa smiled, her heart squeezing tightly with love for her niece in spite of the circumstances. Jenna looked so much like Mercedes that Marissa liked to pretend that Ruben had not fathered her at all. There was little evidence of his tainted blood in her angelic face and that was a blessing. In her opinion, Ruben was not an attractive man and it would've been a cruel joke to curse a daughter with his mug. The fact that she looked so strikingly similar to Mercedes and likewise, herself, had been a point in her favor when she'd made the decision to take her. People would not question that Jenna was her daughter if they moved somewhere where no one knew them.

But to put that plan into play, she'd have to leave everything behind, possibly even travel outside of California to safely pull that off. She sighed unhappily and fell back against the plush sofa, succumbing to a moment of self-pity for the mess she was in.

On impulse, she grabbed her cell phone from her purse. There were seven missed calls from her boss. She listened to the voice mail and cringed when she heard the worry in Layla's voice. Layla had always been a good supervisor to work for at the lab where Marissa had spent the past six years of her life building a reputation for herself. She'd been the recipient of multiple bonuses from the company due to her successful drug trials and she was known for her work ethic. So to drop off the face of the planet was completely out of character and Layla knew it. Marissa could tell her boss was plainly worried sick by the tone of her messages.

One phone call couldn't hurt, she reasoned.

She quickly dialed. Layla picked up on the first ring, no doubt seeing it was Marissa from the caller ID.

"Where are you? What is going on? I went by your apartment and it looks like a hurricane hit it," Layla said all in one breath before Marissa could say a word. Layla's concern sparked an achy feeling in her chest that made it difficult to speak at first. "Marissa? Are you okay? You've got me really freaked out."

"I'm okay." She thought of her apartment, and how Ruben's guys must've trashed it when she split, and swallowed hard. "I need some personal time. My sister—"

"Of course, you do," Layla clucked compassionately. "You should've told me right away. You have plenty of vacation time you can use to get you through this. Did you know our company also pays for grief counseling? You ought to look into that. No sense in paying for benefits you don't use, right?"

"Yeah, I guess so," Marissa murmured, wishing she could tell Layla the truth but knew it was better this way. Besides, Layla was a wonderful boss but they weren't friends in the strictest sense of the word. Somehow telling her boss that she'd stolen a child and quite possibly killed a man might not reflect well on her ability to remain employed. And Marissa was planning to return to her life. Somehow. "Thank you for your understanding. I'm sorry I didn't call. I've been pretty upset these last few days. It just hit me." *Funny, ha-ha, Marissa.* She drew a shuddering breath. "But I'll be okay in a few weeks."

"Who do you want to take over your experiments?" Layla asked, returning to business. Marissa didn't fault her. She had a company to keep running and those drug trials were time sensitive. "How about Danny? Or Veronica?"

She wrinkled her nose at Veronica and quickly agreed to the former. "Danny should be fine. Thanks, Layla."

"Oh, you're most welcome. I feel so bad about

your sister but I'm glad to hear you're okay. When I went by your apartment…well, I immediately thought the worst."

Marissa could only imagine the destruction left behind. It burned to know Layla thought she had wigged out to the extreme and trashed her own apartment but she had little choice but to go along with it. "Extreme grief and too much wine is a bad combination," she murmured, though she grimaced at the lie coming from her mouth.

"Enough said," Layla replied with dry humor. "We've all had a moment where we lose it. Some with less reason than you. Don't worry about it. No one is judging you on this end. I just want to see you back to work when you're ready."

"Thanks," Marissa said, feeling marginally better that she'd tied up at least a few loose ends, but still wishing she could just close her eyes and realize everything had been a terrible dream. But she knew it was real and she had to cover her bases. "Layla, if anyone asks about me, could you keep our conversation under your hat? I just want to decompress for a bit in private."

"You got it," Layla assured her. "You take care, dear."

Marissa ended the call and gazed at her niece happily drooling on a universal remote that probably cost Archer a ton of cash and wondered how exactly she could possibly "take care."

ARCHER RETURNED WITH bags of groceries and various odds and ends that made Marissa wonder if he'd went down each aisle systematically, tossing whatever caught his fancy into the cart. She held up a rubber hot dog that squeaked. "Do you have a dog?" she asked, confused.

Archer scowled and then gestured toward Jenna. "I wasn't sure what she'd play with. I figured something that made noise was a sure bet. Don't kids like to make a racket?"

"I guess so but I think you could've found more suitable toys in the aisle with the kids' stuff, don't you think?"

"I bought everything they had down that aisle but there wasn't much to choose from. So, the kid got a rubber hot dog, too."

His demeanor was gruff but Marissa was silently stunned by his generosity. Looking at the bags littering the living room, he had to have spent a fortune. Her eyes watered but she didn't let the tears fall. She'd cried enough lately but she was ridiculously touched by his attempt to fulfill Jenna's needs. She reached out and tentatively caressed his cheek. He stilled and then shot a quick, suspicious look her way. "What's that for?" he asked.

She removed her hand, wishing she'd just said thank-you and left it at that. But she'd reacted to a gut need to touch him and she'd moved before thinking it through. "I'm sorry," she said, shaking her head. "I just wanted to say thank you. I appreciate all you've done."

Something flitted across his expression but whatever it was he drop-kicked it far and clear within a heartbeat as he said, "Don't thank me yet. We've still got ground to cover and you're not in the clear. I haven't decided what to do with you. I'm not going to sacrifice my career for your screwup. If you remember…it's all I care about."

Her eyes stung as he threw her words at her again. They'd been said in fear of a future that could've left her brokenhearted, so she'd ended their relationship with a clean cut, thinking surgical lines might heal more easily than jagged tears, but she'd been wrong and they both paid the price.

"I'm not asking you to sacrifice anything," she retorted, her pride smarting from his harsh rebuff. "You're the one who told me not to leave. I was prepared to get out of your life this morning, remember?"

"Well, running away is what you're good at. But it's not that simple any longer. By involving me, you involved the FBI. This isn't child's play. We're talking kidnapping here, Marissa. Do you even know what kind of trouble you've gotten yourself into? I'm half tempted to take the kid in myself for your own good. This is going to end badly, I can feel it," he predicted with a growl that sent a shocking shudder tripping down her back.

He cared. He didn't want to admit it, was fighting it, but deep down Archer Brant still had feelings for her. Her breath hitched in her chest and she swallowed the lump rising in her throat. She knew those feelings would never go anywhere but it warmed her shivering soul that they were there.

Archer broke the growing silence with a string of swear words that he didn't even try to censor in spite of Jenna's presence. "I'm going to go shower," he bit off, and then gestured angrily to the bags still unopened. "There are clothes in there for you, too."

ARCHER STOOD UNDER the jet spray, letting the water pelt him on the strongest setting in the hopes that some discomfort would continue to remind him that he was in a mess.

He should've dropped her at the nearest bus station with a handful of cash and sent her on her way. That would've been smart. But since when was he into going the smart route? He turned and leaned into the spray, closing his eyes as the water streamed down his face. He reached forward and grabbed the bar of soap. Why'd she have to look the same as the day she left him? Was it too much to ask that she'd suddenly sprouted an excess of facial hair and a spare tire around her middle? Apparently. Marissa Vasquez had always been his weak spot. And she'd known it. She'd known he wouldn't turn her away—hell, she'd banked on it—and now he was staring down ten different ways to tank his career in one fell swoop. Damn, talk about talent.

But Marissa looked just like she did in his dreams. Long waves of dark hair tumbled down her back and framed her heart-shaped face, drawing attention to the plump and wickedly kissable lips he could still remember tasting. Images from the past, sweaty, sultry and scorching, rose like ghosts to haunt him and his body reacted. His groin tightened with an aching intensity and he stifled a groan at the thick erection that sprang to attention, reporting for duty. God, he wanted her still. After all this time she still managed to twist him in knots.

He gritted his teeth and deliberately jerked the shower knob to cold.

CHAPTER FOUR

RUBEN ORTIZ DRUMMED his long fingers lightly against the top of his desk, silently fuming as he listened to the reports of his men.

"Manny's in bad shape," Raul said, his dark features inscrutable. "The bitch cut him good."

Ruben continued to drum, thinking of Marissa and all the things he wanted to do to her. Things that weren't nice and caused parts to rip and tear. "What does the doctor say?" he asked, his voice calm, hiding the rage inside. "Is he going to live?"

"Only if he gets to the hospital. He needs surgery," Raul answered.

"Tell Dr. Elias to do what he can to make him comfortable. Get him whatever he needs," Ruben said, stilling his fingers to clasp his hands together in front of him as he leaned forward. "No hospital."

"He'll die."

Ruben stared Raul down. "No hospital," he repeated, the light touch of sorrow for his cousin's fate hidden from his voice. His empire was built on the blood of others. He was no stranger to death. Or procedure. "Hospital staff are required to report suspicious wounds to the police. Manuel would never disgrace the family by bringing down *la jura* over this. He has honor and honor lives on even after we die."

Raul slowly nodded, his black eyes narrowing. "You going to make her pay for this insult?"

At that a cruel smile spread from the corners of his mouth as he answered, "In ways you can't even imagine. Find her. Bring her to me alive."

"What of the kid?" Raul asked.

Ruben thought of the child that was of his blood by that faithless whore Mercedes and contemplated how easy it would be to break Marissa using the girl as leverage. His mood lifted. "Bring her, as well. Oh, and, Raul, be careful with the child. She's mine, after all."

WITH JENNA ASLEEP for her afternoon nap, Marissa took the opportunity to get some fresh air. Archer had spent the rest of the morning away from her, cloistered in his study with the door closed, either on the phone or on the computer. A part of her couldn't help but feel like a leper forced into closed quarters with a man who would do anything to avoid contact with her. She tried not to blame him, he hadn't asked for any of this, but her feelings were tender just the same.

She stared out at the mountain vista, watching as

the late-afternoon sun made its slow trek toward the west, and wished she could appreciate the beauty of the view instead of wondering if someone was hiding within the trees, waiting for the right moment to slit her throat.

She didn't think Ruben would find her here but he had resources that she didn't want to fathom and it was possible that there was little that Ruben couldn't get if he put his mind to it.

And he wanted her. He hadn't been subtle in his pursuit once Mercedes ceased to amuse or satisfy him. Marissa shuddered, feeling the sickening slide of his hands on her. A wave of nausea hit her, and she had to force the bile down.

"What's wrong?" Archer asked from behind. She turned to face him and she automatically shook her head in denial. A denial he didn't buy. "You're pale and shaking," he observed, coming closer.

"It's nothing," she lied, her teeth starting to chatter.

He eyed her with suspicion. "You're lying."

"I am not. I just caught a chill is all," she said, trying to move past him, but he caught her arm and pulled her close. The heat from his body seared the skin from her limbs, so that she felt suddenly alive and desperate for more. She wanted to sink into that warmth and pretend she hadn't cut him loose all those years ago and right now they were just enjoying a night in their cabin without danger lurking around each corner. "What are you doing?" she asked softly.

"I wish I knew," he answered, the honesty in his voice cutting her to ribbons. He drew her closer, his face nearing hers, and she felt his breath on her cheek. He smelled of cedar and leather, secret dreams and heartache. She parted her lips, desperately hoping he would kiss her, yet knowing somehow that he would not. He caressed the side of her face and her eyelids closed for a heartbeat, eager for his touch, his comfort, and then he let her go. She opened her eyes and tried her best to hide her disappointment but she'd never been a very good actress so the effort was probably moot. Still it hurt to know that he had such restraint when she was close to begging. She put distance between them. He didn't try to apologize. "Come back in. It might not be safe out in the open," he said, and then returned inside.

ARCHER GRABBED TWO BEERS and when Marissa came in, he handed one to her.

"I don't drink beer," she said, declining.

"Figured you might need a little liquid courage before we begin," he said with a shrug.

She stared. "Before we begin what?"

"Before we begin where we left off."

Her cheeks heated and he knew she was thinking of the moment they shared only seconds ago but he shook his head. "I have to know details, Marissa. You're hiding something and I want to know. No more pussyfooting around. I mean it. You spill the beans or it's over."

She grabbed the neck of the beer bottle. "I guess I'll need that after all," she said.

"Figured you'd change your mind."

She twisted off the top like a pro and took a short swig. He followed, eyeing her above the bottle, noting the shake in her hands hadn't completely subsided but she was trying like hell to make it stop. She grimaced at the taste but didn't complain. "I don't know where to start," she admitted.

"Start at the part where you found Mercedes. What happened after that?"

Her eyes watered and she glanced down, and then she chuckled sadly. "You know it's like my tears are on autopilot. Anytime I think of Mercedes…the waterworks start. I miss her so much."

"Of course you do," Archer said gruffly, looking away so his chest would stop feeling as if an elephant had just used it for an ottoman. "No one expects you to be a rock. But I need to know everything. I think it's safe to say we're not dealing with a bunch of small-town thugs. I've got a guy doing background on this Ruben character but the Oaktown Boyz are no stranger to FBI investigations. You're in some serious shit, Rissa."

"I know that," she said, but she didn't look as frightened as she did a minute ago. Instead, her brows were pulling into a scowl. "I asked you to keep this information to yourself. Who are you telling my business to?"

He held her stare. "Someone I trust," he said, leaving it at that. If she wanted his help she had to let him do things his way. But he figured if he were in her shoes, he'd be touchy, too. "I wouldn't do anything to jeopardize your safety," he said quietly. His admission calmed the storm brewing in those dark eyes and she jerked a short nod.

"If you trust him…I guess I'll trust you."

Her statement caused an ache in his chest that was hard to ignore but he did a fair imitation at least on the surface.

"So how did you—the woman who craves stability and security above all else—" he tried to keep the bitterness out of his voice but he wasn't sure he succeeded for she winced subtly at his comment "—get yourself into this kind of mess?"

She straightened and pushed stray strands of hair from eyes as dark as midnight, and a small sigh escaped. "If you think I don't wonder that myself every moment since Mercedes died, you're mistaken. I'd do anything to go back to my life."

"What happened after you found Mercedes?" he asked again, hating the jealous spurt that spilled over onto his thoughts at her admission. Her work meant everything to her. The fact that she was no different from him should've comforted him in some way but it didn't. It just made him feel rejected all over again.

"I called 911."

"Okay and then what?"

"Well, I had to give a statement to the police," she answered, but the information well trickled to a drip and she was holding on to something she didn't want to share. "And then I went to get Jenna," she finished, averting her eyes.

"And like I said before, I doubt he just handed her over. Plus, you're sporting a nice bruise from someone's fist. Let's start with the easy stuff. Who hit you?"

Her hand went automatically to her lip and her mouth tightened.

"Was it Ruben?" Archer prompted, anger rising again at the thought of Marissa being manhandled by anyone. He forced the red-hot emotion down and focused as if she were just another victim in another case that he was assigned. "Who hit you?" he repeated, this time more forcefully.

"Not Ruben," she answered.

"Then who?"

"His name was Manny…Ruben's cousin."

Archer stilled. "Was?"

Marissa swallowed hard, the telling gesture sending spikes of dread straight to his gut. He had a feeling things were about to go from bad to worse in her world and by proxy his. "What do you mean? Was?"

She looked at him, her eyes misting but she didn't elaborate.

He stared, not quite able to believe what his brain was telling him. "Marissa…did you kill him?"

"I don't know," she answered in a small voice, her fingers nervously fiddling with the beer label on the bottle. She met his gaze, imploring him to believe her, save her, hell probably anything aside from hauling her into the authorities, and he wanted to curse. "It was self-defense," she started, a tear slipping down her cheek. "I swear it. He'd attacked me and there was a struggle…"

Archer had a hard time imagining how Marissa, who stood at a petite five feet four inches tall had managed to overpower a man who was likely taller and stronger unless she'd been prepared for a fight when she walked in there. "Did you shoot him?"

She gave him a wounded look. "You know I hate guns."

"Okay…so what'd you use?"

Marissa hesitated, clearly wishing she could refuse an answer but she knew he wouldn't quit, so she finally relented. "A knife."

"Something small that you could easily conceal," he surmised and she nodded. "So you knew when you walked into that place that it might come down to someone getting hurt."

She shook her head vigorously. "I didn't have a plan per se, I just wanted the knife for protection.

And as it happened I ended up having to use it," she added defensively.

He sighed. "Okay, so you killed this Manny guy…"

She blinked hard. "I don't know…he was bleeding pretty badly…but maybe he lived. Ruben keeps a doctor on staff at the compound for his own personal uses."

"Where'd you stick him?"

"I didn't mean to hurt him," she whispered. "I really didn't. But I was scared and…"

"Where, Marissa?"

She glanced down at the warm beer in her hand. "In the stomach."

"He's dead."

Her head shot up, her expression crumpling.

"Unless the doctor Ruben keeps around has a surgical suite at his disposal…the guy likely bled out."

Marissa put her beer down and dropped her head into her hands. Her shoulders shook as she silently wept. He looked away, not able to watch her pain without feeling it himself. But he was unable to stop from reaching out to her. He tried to ease her pain. "Don't waste your tears on that scum," he said. "I'm not saying what you did was okay but some people deserve what they get."

What he didn't mention was that he was privately glad to hear that the man who'd punched Marissa had taken a knife to the gut. Bleeding out from the stomach was a nasty way to die.

"I didn't mean to kill him," she protested, tears strangling her voice. "I just wanted to get out of there and when he hit me all I could think was 'If I die what will happen to Jenna?' She's already lost so much. I couldn't take the thought that she might lose everyone who would ever love her. Now that Mercedes is gone, I'm all she has."

Knowing what he knew of Marissa, he sensed she was telling the truth, even if she was still skipping out on all the details.

"What was this Manny character doing with the baby?" he asked.

"He was the guard assigned to the nursery," Marissa said, wiping at her eyes and trying to put herself back on track. "He knew I was her aunt so he let me enter. But something must've tipped him off that I wasn't planning to just visit because he came back in to check and that's when he saw me trying to climb out the window with Jenna and her diaper bag."

"You were going to climb out a window with a baby?"

"The nursery was on the ground floor. It wasn't like I was trying to jump from a great height. Anyway, he yanked me back inside and Jenna fell to the floor. She started screaming but before I could try to comfort her, he punched me in the face and I was seeing stars for a minute." Marissa winced at the memory. "And then he kicked me in the ribs. Manny was always a sick bastard. He liked to inflict pain and he hated Mercedes, so when I heard he was guarding the nursery I knew I'd run out of time. I was afraid Manny might hurt Jenna because of who her mother was. But I never expected him to check on me and that was my mistake."

"Why's that?"

"Because…" Her cheeks started to pink and she refused to meet his gaze. That in itself made him worry. Something she'd done was more shameful to her than stabbing a guy in the gut. She squeezed her eyes shut as she answered haltingly, "Because Manny knew I'd—I'd come there at, ah, Ruben's request."

"Hold on. Why would you do that if you thought Ruben killed your sister?"

Tears sparkled in her eyes as she cried, "Because I knew he wanted me and if I pretended to play along…then he would let his guard down long enough for me to get out of town with Jenna."

She'd slept with him. That's what she wasn't saying. What she was dancing around, too ashamed to admit. She'd slept with Ruben to save her niece. He swore under his breath. He stood and walked a short distance before Marissa's voice at his back made him stop.

"Don't you dare judge me," she said, her voice hot but wounded, as well. "I did what I had to do to save her life. You don't know what kind of people Ruben deals with. She was a novelty to him. He wanted her because she was his blood, not because he loved her. He pressured Mercedes to get an abortion and when she refused, he beat her in the hopes that she would lose the baby. You can't tell me that's the kind of man who would make a good father!"

"So the first option you go with is to whore yourself to a man you despise?" he said, turning slowly, anger and pain creating a toxic mixture. He was rewarded with a sharp crack across his jaw. The slap echoed in the room, the only sound between them. He deserved it but he was too angry to acknowledge it. "Feel better?" he asked, his voice tight.

Her nostrils flared ever so slightly as she said, eyes boring into him, "My sister is dead. I'm on the run from a drug lord. And the one man I thought I could count on is looking at me like I'm trash. How do you think I feel?"

She didn't wait for an answer, which was good because he didn't have one for her. She pushed past him and ran up the stairs.

CHAPTER FIVE

MARISSA CUDDLED JENNA and tried to keep from sobbing. It was bad enough that she carried the stain of what she'd done like a brand on her soul but to have Archer look at her in that way...it was more than she could handle.

What had she expected? She wanted to rail at herself for being so naive and hopeful for his unquestioning support. She'd done nothing to garner that from him. She'd pushed him out of her life with the excuse that his job wasn't conducive to the life she wanted. She'd wanted stability and quiet evenings; blessedly normal and suburban, perhaps a child or two, and a membership to the local gym. It was bad enough she had a sister who was constantly putting her on edge, she hadn't wanted a husband who did that to her, as well.

And so she'd pushed him away when he'd been honest about not being able to give her those things because his job was dangerous and unpredictable and there might be nights that he didn't come home at all. She hadn't been able to deal with that future.

But where was she now? Far worse off. And alone with no one to face what was coming her way.

She shuddered and the shake of her body made Jenna twist to stare at her. She tried a smile but it felt more like a grimace and so she stopped. She kissed Jenna's forehead. "I would do anything to keep you safe, *mija*," she whispered. "Anything."

ARCHER WANTED TO HIT something. His rage filled him like noxious smoke. Didn't she realize that he would've helped her if he'd known how desperate she was? Did she think he was such a coldhearted bastard that he'd rather have her spread her legs for some thug than offer to have her back? Her wounded and broken expression haunted him, giving him the answer he didn't want to acknowledge.

He tried to imagine that scenario with him playing the hero for her but he couldn't follow through. She knew him better than he knew himself, apparently.

It shamed him to think he might not have helped. That he might have very well told her to solve her own problems and closed the door in her face. Hell, he didn't know. And she hadn't been able to take the chance, not with that little girl's life on the line. He didn't blame her. Even professionals who do that sort of thing—gamble with the lives of others— screw up and people die.

Just ask Kandy Kane. Oh, that's right. She's dead,

a voice argued with himself, not giving him an inch to breathe.

The detail should've gone down by the numbers. Kandy was only supposed to draw out the perp—a sleazy middleman drug dealer named Vincent with connections to bigger fish—but he'd underestimated Vincent's ability to get at Kandy. Kandy had been killed with a single gunshot wound to the head. In and out. Vincent was never caught and the assignment had failed. Two years of undercover work bled out with their only credible witness. He still saw her open, staring eyes in his imagination, stuck there no matter how many times he was forced to see the shrink.

He paced the kitchen, caught between wanting to apologize for judging Marissa and shouting at her for debasing herself.

Yet, even feeling all these things, he couldn't stop the overwhelming need to console her. His gaze strayed to the upstairs guest bedroom, and he cursed himself as a coward for not being able to just go up there and say the words she needed to hear. *I'm sorry.*

Swearing softly, he disappeared into his study, desperate to find something to occupy his mind so he didn't go and do or say something he'd regret— even more—than he already had.

MARISSA AWOKE TO A soft buzzing and realized her cell phone was vibrating. She frowned as she rubbed the sleep from her eyes to grab the phone. Service here was sketchy, which was something she hadn't minded. It helped to remain cut off from everything to keep from succumbing to the tempting idea of returning.

But as she picked up the phone, she saw a number she didn't recognize. She let it go to voice mail and then hurriedly retrieved the message once it beeped softly.

The voice on the other end, soft and menacing, squeezed the air from her lungs.

"*Mi corazón,* where have you gone? No worries, I will find you. And when I do we shall have many fine hours together. You will beg. I promise. And when you can't take any more, I will let you heal in the finest luxury so when I break you again it will be that much more sweet. See you soon."

Her hand shook as she deleted the message, feeling dirty just for hearing his voice in her ear. Fear snaked its way through her bones and her teeth started to chatter. There was no escaping him. Ruben would find her and when he did... She shuddered, knowing he would do worse than kill her.

She hugged Jenna to her and was helpless to stop the sobs that followed.

THE NEXT MORNING ARCHER awoke earlier than usual with the intent to make amends in some way.

The only way he knew how under the circumstances was to make breakfast. In this, at least, he had some talent.

He wasn't the typical bachelor who couldn't scramble an egg without help but then he wasn't Chef Ramsay, either. He was somewhere in the middle.

He was halfway through the preparations when Marissa came downstairs, carrying Jenna. Her face, pale and drawn, was a direct contrast to the rosy, plump cheeks of her niece.

"I hope you're hungry," he said brusquely, gesturing for her to sit at the bar. She did, watching him curiously with eyes that showed the strain even if she wouldn't admit to it. "You okay?" he asked.

"I didn't sleep well," she murmured, looking away, which was good because he might've winced at her telling statement. He added another handful of cheese to the omelet he was preparing. If he remembered correctly, Marissa liked enough cheese to make it pretty gooey. She smoothed the curls away from the little girl's forehead and pressed an absent kiss there. It was sweet and done without thought, just natural. Something told him that Marissa had been a constant in this child's life long before her mother had exited.

"What was Mercedes like as a mother?" he asked, curious to see if his hunch played out.

Marissa smothered a yawn and shrugged. "The same as she was as a sister. Flighty. Impetuous." She drew herself up and settled the baby more firmly on her lap, a brief smile lighting her lips. "At times generous."

Realizing she might've painted a less than flattering picture, she added, "She loved Jenna with everything she had. But some things don't come naturally to everyone. Just because women can give birth doesn't mean they instinctively know how to mother."

Archer would agree, with one small caveat. Marissa was a born mother. It was in the gentle touch of her hand on the baby's forehead, the sweet curve of her smile when she looked at her niece, the fierce determination to protect at all costs.

Jenna blew a spit bubble, eliciting a genuine smile from Marissa as she wiped it away. Her expression dimmed as she said, "Mercedes tried to be a good mother. But it wasn't until she finally realized that Ruben wasn't a good man to have around a toddler, even if he was her father, that she really started to put Jenna before everything else. Before that…Jenna was…"

"A nuisance?" he supplied. Marissa responded with a faint rise in her cheeks and he knew she hated to admit such a thing about her sister. Speaking ill of the dead…it was just bad form, but facts were facts. He was starting to get a clearer picture of the situation. In her heart, Marissa didn't look at Jenna as a niece…but a daughter. It made perfect sense. No wonder she acted like a mama bear, willing to do anything to save that baby. He set the plate, steaming with a gooey omelet, before her along with the cutlery she'd need. "Some people aren't meant to be parents. It doesn't mean they're bad people," he said softly. Marissa met his gaze and swallowed what was probably a lump of grief and guilt, and slowly nodded.

"It's hard… I loved Mercedes so much but sometimes… I hated her for what she was putting Jenna through with that man. You don't know what he's like, Archer. He comes across as slick and sophisticated but inside he's rotten."

"His kind usually are," he said, eyeing his own omelet without much of an appetite but he sectioned off a piece and ate it anyway. "You don't rise to the top of any heap without skills."

"Skills…interesting way of putting it," she remarked in a soft, wry voice. She pushed at the omelet, probably no more interested in shoveling food down her gullet than he was but food was fuel, and it was never good to go into battle on an empty stomach.

"Eat up," he instructed, and then in a move that surprised them both, winked. "Or you'll hurt my feelings."

At that she chuckled. "Can't have that now, can we?" She took a bite and then smiled around the piece in her mouth as she clearly appreciated his handiwork. "No fair, distracting a woman with good food," she said, cutting a small piece to blow on for Jenna. She tested it with her top lip and then fed it to the baby who accepted it without hesitation. The action tugged at a long-buried part of him that he tried to keep underground. When he'd been starry-eyed in love with her, he'd envisioned such scenes in his head. Her warmth and nurturing spirit called to his lonesome soul in a way that defied explaining. At least it had. He'd have thought after she broke off their engagement he'd have lost those feel-good feelings but no…they were still there, bothersome and confusing.

"Tell me what you know of the Oaktown Boyz gang," he said.

She thought for a moment and then lifted her shoulder. "I don't know much. I tried to steer clear," she said.

Too bad Mercedes hadn't been as smart. "What made Mercedes get the restraining order against Ruben? Had something happened?"

Marissa's expression hardened and he had his answer but he wanted details. For a moment he was afraid Marissa was going to be tight-lipped but she surprised him. "He'd been getting more and more blatant in his attitude toward women and their role in his life, Mercedes included. He liked to pretend that he was like the Oakland version of a rap star. He was never without a woman on his arm. It got to be too much for Mercedes. She confronted him. He didn't like it. Said she insulted him and she needed to be put in her place. Then he beat her almost to death. He put her in the hospital. As soon as she was able, she filed a restraining order and started the proceedings to get sole custody."

"Is there paperwork started on custody?" he asked.

"No." She blew out an unhappy breath. "Ruben got to the attorney before anything was filed. Suddenly, the attorney dropped Mercedes as a client and she was looking for someone new when she was killed."

"Pretty persuasive this Ruben guy," Archer observed, his mind moving in wide circles. "Do you know if he has cops on the payroll, too?"

"I don't know for sure but I suspect he does. Nothing came of the assault on Mercedes even though she pressed charges."

"But an officer came out to take a report?" he asked.

"Yes. One came to the hospital and took her statement there."

Then there should be a record, somewhere. He'd have Rico look into it. An assault on record would go a long way toward establishing motive for Mercedes's death.

"When you gave the police your statement, who did you speak to?"

"I don't remember. Why?"

"Well, if it was a clean cop, there'll be a paper trail. If it was a bad cop, it'll be like it never happened. If the cop who took your sister's statement is the same who took yours and there's no trail...we've found the guy on the take."

"That's great detective work but what good will that do?"

He offered a short smile. "Because it's fun to play with dirty cops. Most of them cave easily when given the right amount of pressure. If we could get this guy to squeal on Ruben, we might be able to crack open his operation and take this scum off the streets for good."

She smiled faintly at that but he could tell she didn't put much faith in the idea. "Maybe," she said.

It made him wonder if he was underestimating this man. He'd certainly made that mistake with Vincent and the shame of his mistake wasn't the worst of it. Kandy's blood was on his hands. He refused to let anything happen to Marissa or Jenna.

Unaware of the turmoil in his head, she glanced at him through black lashes and murmured her thanks for the delicious breakfast but there was something off about the timbre of her voice that immediately put him on alert. She rose, hoisting the baby to her perfectly rounded hip, and said, "I'll help with the dishes if you like but first we both need a good scrubbing."

"Go on ahead, I'll take care of the dishes," he said, wondering at what he saw behind those eyes, ignoring the pulse of desire that flared to life at the thought of her slick, naked body under a jet of water.

"Feel free to use my shower…it's bigger," he said, deliberately giving her his back so he didn't have to look at her. It was bad enough the memory of her body teased his dreams, he didn't need to feed the fire with the real deal.

CHAPTER SIX

RUBEN TOYED WITH THE silver crucifix pendant he'd taken from Marissa's apartment and contemplated how circumstances were slowly slipping out of his control. It'd been a long time since that had happened. He'd almost forgotten what it felt like.

He pursed his lips and curled the pendant in his palm. He didn't like it.

Marissa…so smart, not like Mercedes with her street mouth and whorish ways. Marissa was the kind of woman he would've been proud to have on his arm, and his bed.

But then she had to go and ruin it. She'd tricked him into thinking she wanted to be with him. He should've known better. Marissa had never shown anything but open revulsion for him even when he'd been on his best behavior. That bitch had seen right through him every time. A thin smile followed as he shook his head at the irony. The one woman he wanted was the one woman who couldn't stand him.

She looked at him like he was trash. Her disdain

pricked his pride. He remembered the first time he saw Marissa, so young and fresh, and he'd known…he'd have her. Of course, he knew he'd have to wait. In the meantime, Mercedes had been a pleasant diversion, until she got knocked up. Then she turned into a whining, nagging bitch who made him sick to his stomach at the mere sight of her bloated body.

Raul entered the room and Ruben slowly let the pendant drop to the tabletop. "Tell me you have good news, friend," Ruben said.

"She's not an easy woman to find," Raul started, a frown gathering on his swarthy face. Ruben tried not to let his disappointment show too openly. "Her friends are limited to a few people from work, other than that…she kept to herself."

"Hmm," Ruben murmured in thought, pushing the pendant idly with the point of his finger. "What are they saying at work? How does she explain her absence?"

"Her boss, a woman named Layla, said she needed time to grieve and would be gone a few weeks. But beyond that…she wasn't talking."

Ruben looked up as a thought occurred to him. "Find this Layla woman… Maybe she just needs a little encouragement to share what she knows."

"What are you doing?" Raul demanded, unease in his face. "This woman is driving you loco. Let the bitch go. You aren't playing with a woman from the hood who is easily lost on the streets."

Ruben shot to his feet, menace in his stance as he went toe-to-toe with Raul, who returned the glare. "You questioning me, *cabrón?* If I say I want this woman, it is not for you to ask why."

"You risk too much. There will be questions," Raul said from between gritted teeth. "For what? Let her go. Find a new woman who is less trouble."

Ruben held his stare, and then he smiled abruptly. The action threw Raul off guard, which was what he wanted. Ruben trusted no one, but Raul had always served him loyally. Still, he didn't like the way Raul was watching him as if he was losing his mind. He had to send a message that no one messed with the Oaktown Boyz, and the only way to do that was to bring his beautiful, defiant Marissa back to the family…one way or another. He slapped Raul lightly on the cheek and laughed. "You worry too much. I only want to chat with this Layla woman. No trouble. I'll be the perfect gentleman."

Ruben stepped away, the jocularity leaving his voice as quickly as it appeared. "But if things don't go as planned…I will need you to make sure that there are no loose ends. Can you handle that?"

Raul's mouth tightened and Ruben was struck by how ugly the man was with his pocked face and dark features. Not even a thousand-dollar suit could make that man into anything other than a street thug, yet for some reason this man was growing a conscience over messy details. Damn inconvenient.

He'd have to do something about that.

MARISSA BRUSHED JENNA'S curls before they tangled and then turned to her own. With Jenna playing on the floor, Marissa let her gaze wander the bedroom that adjoined the master bath. It was a strong, masculine room but nothing with too much machismo that screamed I'm afraid of women. She found comfort in its cool wintergreen colors and wood forest accents that were tasteful and classic. Her gaze strayed to the king bed with its luxury bedding—she could tell from the duvet that Archer had dropped some coin—and wondered who else had slid between those sheets after all these years. A man like Archer—who oozed virility—was unlikely to remain celibate. He was a single man, free to sleep with whomever he chose. So why was there a lump forming in her throat? She shook away her thoughts and the accompanying melancholy with blame placed on the situation rather than the events of the past, and tried to think of the positive side of things.

She and Jenna were alive.

How pathetic that she couldn't think of anything else to recommend. She drew a deep, measured breath and rubbed at her nose. She'd always figured herself to be the kind of person who made lemonade out of lemons but right about now...she was plumb out of sugar.

ARCHER GOT OFF THE PHONE with Rico after giving him the newest information about Mercedes and the possible police connection to Ruben Ortiz, and then walked out of the study to see Marissa coming down the stairs with the baby in her arms. His heart contracted at the sight and it took him a full minute to remind himself that it wasn't his right to stare.

God, she broke a man's heart just by standing there. He could still remember the first time he saw her. He'd been doing surveillance on a scumbag dealer who'd liked to hang out at the park near her lab. She'd emerged from the double glass doors, badge pinned to her right breast, with a bag lunch in her hands and a book. At first he'd been mildly amused by the fact that a grown woman had packed a lunch to work. Then, he'd come to realize she did this every day. It seemed something she treasured and enjoyed. She rarely invited others to sit with her but neither was she standoffish or rude. She always had a smile for the waves that came her way or the light conversation that sometimes interrupted her private time. But he'd seen that reserved light in her eyes that told him there was more going on behind those baby browns than she let on. It was the mystery that had spurred him to talk to her.

That day changed his life. He'd never known it was possible to fall in love so quickly. In fact, he'd mocked anyone who tried to say otherwise, but it had taken moments—literally—to fall in love with Marissa Vasquez.

After it was all over he wondered if he wasn't the first schmuck who had bet it all on Vasquez only to lose everything in the end.

"You okay?" she asked, breaking into his reverie. "You have a funny look on your face."

"Did you ever think twice about me after we broke up?" he asked, the shock of the question stunning her into strained silence. He waved away her need to speak. "Forget I asked. The answer is written all over your face," he said, turning to get the hell away from her, angry at himself for letting his mind wander to that forbidden place.

"Archer, wait," she called after him. He spun around so abruptly she nearly ran into him. She'd put the baby down before following him. "Why would you think that I wouldn't?" she asked, her eyes searching his.

"Because it was so easy for you to walk away," he bit out, hating that he sounded like a brokenhearted fool after all these years.

Her eyes watered and she shook her head. "It wasn't easy," she said. "But your lifestyle...I just couldn't deal with it. Stability and my ability to control it in my life was all I had. You threatened everything that was important to me."

"So why'd you agree to marry me?" he demanded.

She looked so sad and nearly as broken as he did as she said, "Because I fell in love with you, you idiot."

It was too easy to look into those eyes and forgive her anything. Even now, angry as hell with the memory of her rejection, he was tempted to just take her into his arms and say to hell with it all and just start over. But she wasn't exactly offering a fresh start. Although she watched from behind a veil of tears that threatened to fall, she wasn't throwing herself into his arms with the promise of a new beginning. She was explaining how she justified breaking his heart into a million pieces for the sake of her need to control her environment. He jerked his hand through his hair, too agitated to say anything more, and finally with a pissed-off groan, stalked away from her.

He needed space.

MARISSA FLINCHED AS the front door slammed behind Archer. Jenna puckered and started to wail. Marissa felt like joining her.

Yet her eyes remained dry. Perhaps she was out of tears. She could hardly believe that. It was more likely that she was becoming accustomed to heartache. Perhaps if she'd stayed with Archer, Mercedes would still be alive. Archer would've been able to keep Mercedes from hooking up with Ruben and all their lives would've been simpler.

But then, she realized with an unhappy start, Jenna would not be here. And Marissa couldn't imagine life without her.

She'd been the first to hold her—Mercedes had been too exhausted to give the infant she'd just brought into the world much thought—so the nurse had given Marissa that precious pink bundle with her full head of inky-black hair and swollen pink mouth that opened and closed like a tiny fish out of water. And then, when Mercedes had been more interested in regaining her figure than attending to the overwhelming needs of an infant, Marissa had used her accumulated vacation time to care for her.

No, she couldn't imagine life without Jenna. Even if it meant dealing with Ruben.

And on the nights she'd rocked Jenna through her bouts of colic, she thought of her own mother and how much she would've loved being a grandmother. She sang songs she remembered from her mother and hummed wordless tunes that floated from her memory even if she didn't remember how she knew it. For all intents and purposes, she was Jenna's mother and nothing would ever change that.

ARCHER WAS NOT QUITE sure who he was mad at—himself or Marissa—but he was hot and he knew if he didn't get some air to clear his head, he'd explode.

The tension coiled inside him was a dangerous thing. He needed an outlet. They were trapped in close quarters together, the attraction he still felt for Marissa causing him to act out in ways that were humiliating for them both, and yet, a part of him was secretly glad she came to him for help.

He was sick in the head.

What were they doing? Aside from ripping open old wounds that had finally scabbed over? Damn it.

His ears pricked at the sound of a vehicle coming down his dirt driveway and he bolted for the house.

"Arch—" Marissa started as he came inside, an apology clearly in her expression but he didn't have time for that.

"Get upstairs," he ordered. At her questioning expression, he explained quickly. "Car's coming. I don't get a lot of visitors. Now get upstairs and keep the baby quiet."

Fear flooded her gaze and she scooped up Jenna with sure hands before running up the stairs to disappear in the guest bedroom.

Pulling the gun from the sideboard drawer, he took position to the right of the door, waiting. The vehicle stopped at the front of the house. Footsteps crunched the loose gravel and climbed up the porch steps. A heavy knock sounded.

"Who is it?" he called out.

"It's me, you son of a bitch. Now open the door," a familiar voice shouted, and Archer drew back, stunned.

Archer threw open the door and stared. "How the hell—"

Josh Halvorsen stared him down, pissed as all get out, and looking like he wanted to put his fist through his face. "It's a small town. There's only one Realtor in town. All it took was a little conversation with Janelle Grafton to find out that you had let the house sitter go. Word spread quick that you were back in town. I wondered if you had the balls to give me a call. Apparently, you don't."

Archer drew back, insulted, but he didn't have the option of brawling it out with Josh on his front porch, so he gestured for the man to come inside. Josh followed, a frown still on his face, and Archer shut and locked the door. "A little paranoid, aren't you?" he asked, eyebrows raised at Archer's actions. "Everything all right?"

"A minute ago you wanted to punch my lights out, now you're concerned about my welfare? Pick a side, Josh. It was never like you to be wishy-washy."

Josh's face darkened. "I'm still pissed at you but that doesn't mean I don't care if you're in some kind of trouble."

"I'm touched."

"Man, you're a dick. That much hasn't changed."

Archer resisted the urge to glance upstairs, but he

sure as hell hoped Marissa stayed put. He wasn't in a frame of mind to start explaining. "I meant to call," Archer started, but he stopped. Josh deserved better than that. He wasn't going to lie. "You're right. I am a dick. Things have been pretty messed up lately and after I unloaded on you the last time we spoke…I figured you probably didn't want to talk to me so I just kept my distance," he said, the admission feeling good.

"You said some harsh things."

If he'd had less pride he would've hung his head in shame. "Yeah, there's no excuse for it. All I can say is I was lashing out at the closest target. It wasn't right but I can't take it back."

"No, you can't. But you can apologize," Josh offered.

"And you'd accept that?" Archer asked.

Josh shrugged. "Try me."

Archer shook his head. The conversation was surreal, but he supposed it wouldn't hurt to give it a whirl. "Okay, I'm sorry, man, for being such a jerk. It was uncalled-for and there's no excuse for my behavior."

"Not bad for a guy who hates to admit when he's wrong," Josh said, then surprised Archer with a smile. "Apology accepted. You were hurting and I get that. I remember what it feels like to nurse a broken heart. What upset me was the fact that you just disappeared. No word, nothing."

"My job made it easy to do that."

"Yeah…I know. That's why when I heard that you were home—" Archer winced at the word *home* and Josh reached out to grasp his shoulder, surprising him with the gesture as Josh wasn't the touchy-feely type. "This is your home. There are people who love you here in this town. My family included. My mom was worried sick."

Archer thought of Mary Halvorsen and a warm feeling followed. That woman was tough as nails but she had a heart that wouldn't quit. Not even when a kid from the wrong side of the tracks tried everything possible to push everyone away. She'd shoved food down his throat when he was too proud to admit there was nothing to eat in his own house and bought him jeans when the ones he was wearing were in shreds. Not to mention the shoes. A wave of shame made him ask, "Is everything okay with your mom? Everything good on the home front?"

Josh nodded. "Things are good. Mom would love to see you again."

"I'm sorry…things are complicated right now."

Josh made a face. "She loves you like a son, which—"

"Archer?"

Both men turned at the sound of Marissa's voice. Damn. This is what he'd hoped to avoid.

"Marissa?" Josh's look of surprise was mirrored

in his voice. Then, Josh turned to Archer. "Something you want to share?"

"No," he answered but knew he'd end up doing just that. With a disgruntled sigh, he gestured for Marissa to come downstairs. She disappeared for a moment and reappeared with the baby in her arms. Josh's eyes widened and then his stare swiveled to him, and Archer felt the need to defend himself. "It's not what it looks like," he grumbled. He might need a beer—or several—to get through this reunion.

"Josh…" Marissa murmured, a hesitant smile in her voice. "It's been a while. How have you been?"

"Can't complain. Me and Tasha adopted a baby boy from Punta Gorda. But what about you?" He gestured to the baby and, as always, her gaze softened with pure joy.

Archer cut in before Marissa could answer. "Like I said, things are complicated. Marissa is…visiting for a few days."

"Ah," Josh said, but he wasn't buying it. Still, he chose to go along with the story for the time being and Archer was relieved. "How about a beer? I see your manners haven't gotten any better in the three years you've been away. Miller, if you've got it."

There was no point in refusing, Josh seemed ready to air their dirty laundry and he wasn't about to leave until they patched things up. That had always been something Archer appreciated—if only secretly—

about his friend. If it hadn't been for Josh's stubborn refusal to take no for an answer, Archer would've been one lonely son of a bitch when they were growing up.

"One beer," Archer growled and stalked into the kitchen.

MARISSA WAS EMBARRASSED by Archer's attitude, though why she felt compelled to feel anything on Archer's behalf she didn't know. But she did know that Josh had been Archer's best friend all through high school and beyond and it wasn't right for Archer to be so short with him without cause.

When Archer left the room, she caught Josh's keen eye settling on the faint bruising along her lip and she felt the overwhelming urge to hide. Instead, she met his questioning stare head-on. She wasn't the kind of person to run and hide—even when she should—so why start now? "It wasn't Archer," she said softly, and he started, obviously ashamed that she'd caught him speculating. "I came to him for help."

"What's wrong?" he asked. "Anything I can do?"

She smiled. Archer had told her the stories of practically growing up in the Halvorsen household and how they could never resist a friend in need. It warmed her just a little to know that he considered her a friend. "Thanks. I wouldn't want to get you involved. It's bad enough I've dragged Archer into it," she admitted, moving to the sofa to sit. She gave a toy to Jenna and then settled back with a sigh. "Things have changed a lot since I saw you last."

She'd met Josh and Tasha Halvorsen when Archer had finally brought her to Emmett's Mill after much needling. She'd wanted to know more about the man she'd fallen in love with. Archer wasn't the kind to share background information lightly. She figured by seeing where he grew up she might get a little more insight into the man. She hadn't thought it would be so difficult to get him to agree. After some time, he'd finally caved but he hadn't been happy about it. She'd been enchanted with the lovely scenic town but she'd known right away that his memories weren't all great. While he clearly loved Josh in a brotherly way, going home had made him edgy.

Perhaps that hadn't changed. She wondered why he stayed at all.

"So…Marissa…what have you been up to? I didn't realize you and Archer had kept in touch after…you know, the breakup," he stumbled a little and his cheeks colored but she forgave him with a smile. It was awkward for everyone. She wasn't going to make it worse.

"We didn't. I surprised Archer by showing up. This is my niece, Jenna. I know you noticed the bruise. It's okay, it's hard to miss. My sister was killed recently and we needed a safe place. Archer was the first person I thought of."

Archer appeared with two beers and, after handing

Josh his, cracked his own. Marissa looked to him, trying to gauge his mood but aside from an overall tightening of his features, he was unreadable. She did sense that he and Josh had a lot of catching up to do. Rising, she gathered the baby and announced they were going to take a short nap. "It was nice to see you again, Josh," she said with a genuine smile and then left the men to their conversation. By the looks of it, Archer wasn't looking forward to it.

CHAPTER SEVEN

BOTH MEN WAITED UNTIL Marissa was behind closed doors before speaking. Then Josh didn't waste time.

"Who hit her?"

Archer's mouth tightened and it was a long moment before he answered. He didn't really want Josh involved but he supposed an abridged version was acceptable.

"Her sister ran into some trouble, got tangled up with the wrong people. She was killed recently and Marissa got caught in the cross fire."

"She going to be okay?" Josh asked.

Archer shrugged, he didn't know the answer to that. He didn't even know how to help her yet. Or if he could help her at all. The whole situation screamed complicated. "I'm just giving her a place to crash for the time being," he said, making it sound as if he really wasn't concerned with the details of her problems. Given the way things ended between them, Josh should've bought it. Yet, the man was looking at him as if he knew there was more to the story.

"Someone smacked her good. I imagine she looked pretty roughed up when she first got here," Josh commented between swigs. "Must've been a shock to find her on your doorstep."

"You have no idea," he muttered. More like a nightmare and a dream come true all in one. How many times had he privately wished that she'd suddenly change her mind and want to get back together again in the days after their breakup? More than he cared to admit. It made him feel pathetic and weak. He swallowed a mouthful of beer and then let out a satisfying belch. "So, Halvorsen…you didn't come to shoot the shit. So let's get down to brass tacks. Apology or not, you're here to give me what for and I deserve it so let 'er rip."

Josh actually smiled and tipped his beer. "I was never one to hold a grudge. Like I said, I guess you had your reasons for acting like a total asshole. You're sorry and I believe you. So seal the deal and come have dinner with us tomorrow night."

"I don't know if that's a good idea," Archer hedged for a number of reasons, not all of them attributable to Marissa's situation. Josh may be able to forgive him for being such a jerk but he wasn't ready to forgive himself. Just seeing Josh again made him flinch with shame.

"Why are you letting me off the hook so easily?" he demanded. He wanted some kind of penance, otherwise how could he ever earn the man's friendship back? At Josh's perplexed expression, he rose and walked to the window, glancing about his property as a habit but also to avoid the face-to-face stuff that he really sucked at. "I blamed you for a long time, even though it wasn't your fault in the least. How can you forgive me?"

"Because you're my best friend, Arch."

Josh's solemn answer deflated him. He turned. "Just like that?" he said.

"Yeah. Just like that. We've known each other a long time. Do you know how I know you're a good friend? Because it doesn't matter how long it's been since we've seen each other. It still feels the same between us. When I was married to Carrie, we hardly saw each other. I was in Stockton and you were off playing soldier boy. But that didn't matter, did it?"

"Of course not."

"Well, so we had a rough patch and it lasted a few years. Standing here right now, it doesn't feel any different than it ever did. That's how I know."

Archer was horrified to feel moisture pricking his eyes. Good grief. "Well, shit," he mumbled, mostly to himself. Country logic got him every time. He looked up and found Josh watching him with a warm grin. He rolled his eyes and said, "Don't you try to hug me, Halvorsen. You know I don't swing that way."

Josh cracked up. "Yeah, well, that's good. Tasha doesn't like to share," he said, adding, "And if I ever did swing that way, sorry, buddy, but you wouldn't be my first choice. I know too much about you. There's no mystery."

They shared a smile and it felt good, even if Archer's felt a little rusty. "You're a good man, Halvorsen. How'd I ever get so lucky?"

Josh shrugged. "Dunno, but don't push it. Next time you decide to go AWOL and mad dog on me, you're on your own. Now tell me what's really going on with Marissa."

Archer sighed. He wanted to…but he didn't want to put Josh and his family at risk. He had a bad feeling about this situation with Marissa and it had nothing to do with the fact that he might still be in love with her.

IT WAS SOME TIME before Josh left, and as Marissa came downstairs with Jenna, she wondered what mood she'd find Archer in.

She was surprised to find him in the kitchen.

"You're a regular Rachael Ray, aren't you?" she teased lightly, coming around the bar. She gestured to the fixings and asked, "What's on the menu?"

"Nothing fancy, just your basic meat, potatoes and greens."

"Sounds good to me," she said, moving past him to make Jenna a bottle. "So, it was nice to see Josh again," she started, hoping to open the conversation.

"Yeah, it was," Archer agreed, and then moved to

start chopping the tomatoes for the salad. He shot her a quick look and said, "I didn't give him details of your situation."

"Oh. Thank you. I mean, I trust Josh, he seems like a good man, but I wouldn't want his family to get wrapped up in this mess."

"My thoughts exactly," he agreed, sliding the tomatoes into the bowl and moving on to the cucumbers.

"You seem like something is bothering you," she commented, frowning as he jerked the lettuce with more force than needed. "You don't have to cook for us, you know," she said. "I'm perfectly capable of putting food together."

"It's not you," he said.

"Then what is it?"

He stopped, the knife clenched in his hand. Then he swore and put the knife down before looking at her. "When we broke up…I said some pretty bad things to Josh. Things he didn't deserve after everything he's ever done for me."

"Why would you do that?" she asked, confused.

"Because I was a mess when things ended," he admitted softly. Her insides quivered and she knew the person he had wanted to lash out at was her but she hadn't been available. She bit her lip and remained quiet. When he realized she wasn't going to say anything to his confession, he shook his head and went back to the vegetables. "Well, I screwed up and took it out on my best friend because I was jealous of his happiness. How good of a best friend am I? The man is there for me my entire life and I go and dump on him because I'm so messed up. Nice. Maybe it's a blessing we didn't work out. It's obvious I don't have it in me to take another person's feelings under consideration."

"Stop," she ordered, surprising him with her vehemence. She wasn't going to listen to this pity-party, not from him. "You're not a bad person, so stop trying to pretend to be one. You reacted to a situation that was emotionally hurtful. That's it. And Josh forgave you, so just stop."

He turned to Marissa, his expression haunted and bleak, more so than the situation warranted, in Marissa's opinion, which made her wonder what he wasn't telling her. "You don't know who I am anymore, Marissa," he said. "I've done things…hurt people."

"Like what and who?" she asked, startling him with her demand. "You were a soldier who went to war. I told you then and I'm telling you now, what you did in the service of your country is simply that. As far as what you do in your job now…well, it's not like you work a normal nine to five. I suppose there's a certain amount of occupational hazard. We've both done and said things we've regretted over the past three years, Archer. Don't you think of all people, I would understand that?"

He met her questioning gaze and he held it for a long moment. She wanted to smooth away the lines that creased his forehead and make him understand that he didn't have to shoulder the world, even if someone asked him to. But that wasn't her right any longer. And she needed his protection, so she was doing the very thing she knew she shouldn't. It was a twisted situation and there was no help for it. So they had to make the best of it, scars and all. Jenna fussed and tugged at her pant leg. Marissa bent to pick her up.

"You're good with her," Archer commented, almost wistfully. "You're a good mother. I always knew you would be."

The breath hitched in her chest. It was painful to hear him say that when they had talked often about children in playful, meandering conversations that had started with laughter and ended with passion. How far away they were now from that time in their lives. Realizing the moment had stretched on too long, she simply smiled at the compliment, not ready to let him know how much she still cared…and wished wholeheartedly that she'd made a different choice when it could've mattered and made a difference for everyone.

LATER THAT NIGHT WHEN Jenna was asleep, Marissa went to Archer's door and knocked softly. There were things that needed to be said and if she didn't at least try, she might lose the tenuous grip she had on her sanity. The moments ticked on, increasing the pressure in her chest as she considered that he either was avoiding her or was asleep, but as she lifted her curled fist to knock again, the door opened.

She swallowed the knot in her throat at the sight of him. Bathed in soft light from the small bedside lamp and wearing nothing but a pair of soft flannel pajama bottoms, she tried not to focus on the ridges of hard flesh that filled the landscape of his chest and abs and made her fingers tingle with the need to touch. He was a man of epic proportions, in every sense. He'd always made her feel distinctly feminine with his bulk beside her, on top of her, inside her. She wrestled with a shudder as he watched her warily. "Something wrong, Rissa?" he asked, the low pitch of his voice touched with concern made her ache inside for something that didn't belong to her. The sound of her nickname on his tongue made her melt.

"I...wanted to talk with you," she stammered, averting her eyes from his body so she could think clearly. She wondered briefly at the thick, white bandage covering a section of his shoulder but she was too wrapped up in her own tangled thoughts that she pushed it away for the time being.

He grabbed a shirt from the back of the chair nearest the door and pulled it on. She flicked a look of gratitude his way, though he surely didn't realize his near naked-body made her squirm in a way that had nothing to do with modesty. He paused, then gestured for her to come inside. "Something has been bothering me and I need to get it off my chest," she said, once she was inside.

His squint said *Oh, God, there's more to this mess,* but he didn't comment, just waited for her to start talking.

But her throat seemed closed and actually getting the words out became difficult at best. Her distress was evident and his expression gentled. Pulling her to the bed, he said, "Whatever it is, we'll figure it out. I have a friend in the Bureau who's chasing down some leads on this Ruben guy—"

She interrupted him with a shake of her head. "It's not about Ruben. It's about you and me."

ARCHER FELL SILENT AT her admission, his thoughts jumbled as he wondered what she could mean. He didn't want to jump to conclusions, though it was hard not to. A part of him was tempted to go on the defensive but he tried to rein that urge in, along with the other urges that were making tapioca of his brain.

Didn't she know how beautiful she was? How she made him want to take her into his arms and make her his again? The sharp white dress shirt he gave her to sleep in—his T-shirts would've clung to her every curve—went past her knees, but her legs, tanned and toned, were bare to her coral-painted toes. The shape of her breasts were hidden from him by the oversize shirt but he had no trouble recalling their firm weight in his hand, the taste of the dusky nipple in his mouth.

Her hair fell in loose waves down her back, the ends curling softly in a wild tangle that he knew would feel like silk sliding through his hands. He remembered how she liked to be touched, kissed. The memory of her scent taunted and teased in the cruelest of ways, made his skin tighten all over in eager anticipation of something he couldn't have, shouldn't want.

"What is it?" he asked, his voice harsher than he'd intended, feeling like a car hurtling down a freeway into oncoming traffic with the brake line cut. His body heated with the desire he barely kept restrained and he realized, too late, that he should've moved this conversation out of the bedroom, somewhere that wasn't conducive to taking her down onto the goose-down comforter and loving her until she couldn't breathe. But God help him, he couldn't get himself to commit to the words. Instead he held them back and waited in willful torture for whatever would come next.

Her eyes were troubled and he wondered what could compel her to come to him in the dead of night. Whatever it was, it was eating her up inside and for that he wished he could just ease her mind. But he didn't get the chance for she chickened out. "Never mind," she whispered, turning to bolt but he wouldn't let her.

"Not so fast," he said, easing his hold on her but not quite letting go. He could feel the wild thrum of her pulse under the pads of his fingertips, further proof of her anxiety. His thumb rubbed lazy, gentle circles on the soft skin in his possession while he looked her in the eye. "Say what you came to say," he said.

"It's not important," she stammered. Her tongue snaked out to moisten the plump bottom lip that Archer found maddeningly tempting. The house was quiet and dark. He was curious…and hungry.

"It's the middle of the night," he reminded her quietly, his gaze lingering on the proud high cheekbones. "Whatever it is obviously couldn't wait until morning, so just go ahead and say it."

"I changed my mind," she said, gasping as he pulled her to him.

A slow smile molded his mouth. She came with little resistance but he could feel her heart slamming hard, and those gorgeous drown-in-me eyes were wide and dilated, betraying her as readily as her lush mouth when it opened slightly. Yet no protest followed. She was like a beautifully trapped bird and he wanted to keep her forever.

"Archer—"

"Too late, baby," he all but growled, knowing that she thrilled at his authority even if she resisted it. It'd been a game they'd played often and he was quick to recall the rules from his memory. "You knew the minute you came to my door what you were looking for," he said. *And I'd be a fool to let you go.* Still, he waited a millisecond for her refusal. As he knew it wouldn't, nothing of the sort fell from her lips.

Slowly, he slid both hands down to her perfect ass and filled each palm, lifting her to his mouth even as he bent to meet her. She opened on a gentle gasp and he pressed her harder against him, taking her mouth with deep, lazy yet possessive strokes of his tongue against hers.

This is what his dreams were made of—him and Marissa pressed against each other, wanting, needing, taking, giving—and it filled him with heady desire that she was real and not just a figment of his memory.

He'd planned to take things slow but there was a craving so deep, his bones ached, and soon he wasn't sure who was in control any longer.

He lifted her with a groan born of need and she wrapped her legs around him, pressing the hot core of her against his midsection. He nearly lost all sense of reason, not that he had a lot at this point, but he clung to whatever he could to keep himself in check. A kiss wasn't going to hurt anyone, he thought with ragged justification. A kiss…one hot scorcher of a kiss, but just a kiss.

But then somehow they landed on the bed and as her nimble fingers grazed the hard, straining length that he was trying his damndest to keep under control, he bit back a groan and knew he was screwed.

How did it come to this? Marissa didn't know but she was starving for his touch. There were too many layers of clothing between them, she thought, jerking at the soft material that kept him from her. He ripped at the expensive dress shirt she wore and she laughed as buttons popped, baring her breasts to his hot and wild gaze. He looked like a man who'd died and gone to heaven. Or a man about to consume the best meal he'd ever eaten. The thought sent a riotous shudder through her body as she moved to claim his mouth as he'd claimed hers.

His touch burned away the rot of what she'd done with Ruben and seared new memories into her brain that she gladly embraced.

Archer's tongue tangled with hers and she moaned against his lips, barely able to catch her breath as he assaulted her in the most wonderful way possible and her panties were suddenly gone along with his pants and T-shirt.

Oh, how she'd missed this magical feeling between two people who couldn't get enough of one another. No, it wasn't that simple. She'd missed Archer. Desperately.

They rolled and she went on top. His hands cupping and kneading her breasts, rolling the pebbled tips of her nipples with hands that were rough and gentle at the same time. She gasped as spikes of desire sent warm heat south and she slicked quickly with moisture, eager—no, frantic—to feel him inside her.

But before she could impale herself on that wonderful, rigid length of his, he rolled her again and she only had a moment to sulk as he threw her legs over his shoulders and buried his face in that hot, pulsing center, flicking and teasing the coiled tension building inside her. She breathed deeply, twisting the soft, pillowy comforter in her fists, as a cry built in her throat. Her belly quivered and her muscles trembled as a wave of clenching sensation made her suck a wild breath as she came so hard, she was limp and barely able to catch her breath when it was over.

Oh, yesss. Little shock waves of pleasure shimmered through her body in pleasant waves and tingles but she had little opportunity to simply lie sated and weak. Archer's tight, feral expression as he loomed over her sent a dark thrill chasing after the orgasm that wrung her out, and she grinned up at him, daring him to push her to that edge again.

Thank God, Archer was never one to back down from a challenge.

ARCHER'S HANDS SHOOK with his need to fill her body. Her skin glowed with a thin sheen of sweat and the musk of her desire filled the air. It was like heaven.

She was ready, pliant and willing. She clung to him and whispered soft erotic words guaranteed to send him driving into her. That's exactly what she wanted and he was more than willing to give it to her. He gritted his teeth, pausing only long enough to rip open the condom package and sheath himself before slipping into her with one bone-melting thrust that sent a wild shudder screaming down his body as his brain screamed more and he mindlessly obeyed.

She wrapped her legs around him and he buried his face against the sweet skin of her neck, sucking in the soft flesh with enough pressure to earn a gasp but not enough to leave a mark, and moved with her in perfect rhythm. This woman was everything to him, his heart sang, as his body claimed hers. And when he came in hot spurts that hurtled out of his body, his mind had little time to balk at the simple message his heart was calling out.

That would come soon enough.

CHAPTER EIGHT

IT WAS SEVERAL HOURS later when Marissa slid from Archer's bed, rumpled, deliciously sore in all the right places, and suffering from a major case of Mother-Mary-have-you-lost-your-mind? She snatched her discarded shirt from the floor, remembering too late that the buttons had all been ripped off in their frenzy, and simply tucked the ruined shirt against her sides as she tried to tiptoe from the room.

Archer awoke as she reached the door.

"Where you going?" he inquired sleepily. She'd forgotten how easily he awoke, a remnant from his military training.

She turned, her hand still on the door. "The baby...I can't leave her alone. She might roll off the bed or something. I'd feel more comfortable being with her," she whispered, glad for the dark of the room so he wouldn't have to watch her walk of regret. She'd never do anything to hurt him—again—but that's exactly what she'd end up doing if he read her face right now. He'd take it the wrong way, they'd end up arguing, and then she might lose the one ally she had in this whole mess.

But he seemed to accept her answer and she slipped from the room, relieved yet weighed down by the knowledge that this was likely a one-time deal.

She hurried to the guest bedroom and after a quick wash in the bathroom, she climbed into bed, careful not to jostle the baby.

Archer, she said his name in her head and closed her eyes but he was still there. Sex had been a mistake. When the light of morning hit, he'd come to that realization, too. She'd have to be ready for it so it didn't tear her to shreds. But it'd been so wonderful, so perfect. Why'd it have to be wrong? She squeezed her eyes tighter but the moisture welling managed to escape anyway. A physical ache bloomed in her chest and she recognized it for what it was—a wounded heart.

She'd pushed Archer away. She had no right to hope for more. Besides, what if he was only pretending to get close to her to stab her in the back later? It would only be what she deserved. She shuddered. The thought was too much to bear.

Marissa buried her head in her pillow and quietly wept.

ARCHER AWOKE A LITTLE later than usual but still before the sun crested the horizon. God, he felt good. There was a spring in his step, a smile on his face, and his muscles had that great worked-over feeling he got after an intense gym session. His first thought was of freshly squeezed orange juice and how good it would taste sliding down his throat.

Bounding from the bed, a whiff of last night's activities assailed his nostrils. His grin widened and he considered waking Marissa with a kiss but as he walked the hallway toward the guest bedroom he realized there was movement downstairs. Peering over the banister, he saw Marissa's dark head as she sat on the sofa, thumbing through an old *Car and Driver* magazine.

"Good morning," he said, coming down the stairs. "Sleep good?"

"Not really," came her answer, sending a discordant note through his mind that signaled bad news was coming. That feel-good, happy mood began to leak out of him like helium through a pinpricked balloon. "We need to talk," she said as she tossed the magazine to the coffee table.

And there went the last of the good feelings.

"I think this is going to require coffee first," he grumbled. Why did everything good in his life have such a short shelf life, he wanted to know. Josh had always accused him of being a pessimist, but really, Archer considered himself more of a realist, and so when he finally sat across from Marissa, he wasn't surprised when she started the conversation with an unhappy frown.

"Archer, you know I care about you," she began in what sounded a lot like the speech she gave when she broke their engagement. His hands curled around the hot cup, but he didn't take a drink. He watched her as she struggled with the right words needed to crush him to dust and wondered why she was trying to tiptoe around it. He leaned back and slowly raised the cup to his lips, his gaze boring into hers, daring her to continue. She faltered for a moment but kept going. "I've made a lot of mistakes as of late and I think last night—"

"Was a mistake," he cut in, unable to let her finish. He could take a bullet without crying but listening to Marissa filet him alive with those soft words and brown doe-eyes did a number on him that he wasn't willing to entertain again. He shrugged away her frown at his interruption and continued. "Yeah, I get that. Is this really what this conversation is going to be like? Because if it is, let me save you the trouble. I get it, Marissa. You were horny and wanted to relive some old times. Great. Same here. But don't worry, one roll in the sack isn't going to make me drop to my knees and propose. I made that mistake once and I don't make the same mistake twice, so stop worrying that pretty little head of yours over little ol' me. Okay? Okay. Great. Glad that's over. I'm going for a run."

He finished the coffee, burning the hell out of his mouth in the process but welcoming the pain, and sprinted up the stairs, eager to get the hell away from her. A run would do him good, clear his head of the sappy, poisonous feelings that he'd been marinating in mere hours ago and put his thoughts back on track.

He was changed and ready within minutes. But as he descended the stairs, adjusting his iPod on his biceps and fitting his earbuds into place, he was confronted by one angry Latina.

"What the hell is wrong with you?" she asked, her voice trembling with rage and something else just under the surface. If he didn't know better he'd have said it was hurt feelings, but the woman had a chunk of ice where her heart should be, so that couldn't possibly be it. He moved past her and she followed. "Don't turn your back on me, Archer. This isn't finished until I get my say. You don't get to dump all over me and then go on your way, happy as a clam. Do you hear me?"

He turned. "Marissa, I think the entire forest can hear you. You're getting a little shrill. Dial it down, if you wouldn't mind."

"Well, I do mind and I won't dial it down," she returned, a note of hysteria coloring her voice, her eyes flashing with righteous anger. "You have some nerve to treat me like this. Is this how you treat everyone who comes to you for help?"

"Of course not. As a rule I don't sleep with the people I'm assigned to," he said casually. Inside he was as angry as she was on the outside but he wasn't ready to let her see how her rejection had cut him. "But then, you weren't assigned to me, either. You're more like a freelance gig so all bets are off, right? Besides, what are you all jacked up about, sweetheart? We both got what we wanted, no harm no foul, and I'm still going to help you out as best as I can so stop looking at me like you want to commit a felony."

Tears sparkled in her eyes and her mouth quivered. He already felt rotten inside. What was one more load to carry? "Is that all?" he asked.

She lifted her chin before she spoke, taking the time to make sure her voice didn't betray anything more than her face had already and said, "Thanks for clearing things up for me. You're a jackass and I was wrong to think you might've been the one. You see, I thought I was the one who had made the mistake letting you go, but now I realize it was a blessing. You're as black inside as Ruben. It just took a lot longer for me to see it."

She turned stiffly away from him and then walked up the stairs, her shoulders as straight as her spine, and then disappeared behind a closed door.

Temptation prompted him to follow her, his heart begged for him to apologize, but his head forced his feet to move in the opposite direction. The drill sergeant in charge sent him out the door, running for control of his life.

MARISSA'S EYES WERE swollen and she'd tried commanding the tears to stop but they came anyway. It seemed all she'd done in the past week was bawl. She was sick of herself, her weakness, her own failings. It burned to know that she and Mercedes had the same tendency to make bad choices when it came to men. She'd always prided herself on not following the same path as her older sister yet the facts were clear. Mercedes had fallen helplessly in love with a criminal; she'd given her heart to a bastard. The end result was similar with one small difference—she wasn't dead.

How could she have been so blind when it came to Archer? She packed what little belongings she'd brought with her and started with Jenna's things.

But she couldn't think straight any longer and that extended to tasks as simple as throwing clothes into a bag. She crawled into the bed, thankful Jenna was still fast asleep, and curled up to the one person she'd do anything for and knew the sacrifice would be worth it.

Perhaps Archer considered this payback for how she ended things. Perhaps he thought his flippant treatment was justified. He'd be wrong. He had no idea how she'd already suffered. And it was simply cruel of him to try and carve more out of her than what had already been taken.

If he knew… A soft hiccup followed and she shut down her mind, needing sleep. And God help her…a new life.

ARCHER RAN. HIS FEET HIT the paved road, creating a staccato beat that kept him going even when his lungs burned and his shoulder screamed from the activity. So much for babying it. Sorry, Doc.

Why couldn't he push Marissa from his mind? That crushed look on her face that she'd tried to hide with indignation kept coming back to slap him. She was right. He was a jackass. And a coward. That's what she didn't know. God, he'd been terrified of that pain of rejection so he'd drop-kicked her first. What a pussy. What a grade-A asshole. He hadn't given her the chance to even say what she'd been trying to tell him. What if he misconstrued the whole thing? What if she'd been working up the nerve to say something that had nothing to do with kicking him to the curb? A sick feeling lodged in his gut that had nothing to do with the fact that he'd just pounded out ten miles after a long hiatus from his usual exercise routine. Well, it might have something to do with it, he thought regretfully, slowing to heave his guts out against the base of a pine tree. Coffee and not much else splashed to the ground and he realized he'd pushed things too far.

And he wasn't just talking about the run.

Good thing he had a long way back to figure out how to fix things.

MARISSA HAD FINISHED feeding Jenna and cleaning up the mess when Archer walked through the door, looking like hell. The brisk spring air had put roses in his cheeks but against the white of his skin it only looked garish. He was breathing heavily and headed straight for the kitchen sink. She watched, curious in spite of her decision to tell him exactly how he could shove his help up his ass, as he dunked his head and drank straight from the tap. She blinked. That was unlike Archer.

"Are you all right?" she asked, cursing herself for being a sucker. In a past life she was probably a victim of Jack the Ripper. "Does this have anything to do with your shoulder injury?" she asked, remembering the white bandage from last night.

He simply looked at her. *Fine. Jackass.* She stiffened and picked up the baby so she could get everything loaded in the car but he stopped her when she reached the base of the stairs.

"I'm sorry."

His voice, hoarse and raspy, made her turn. "Excuse me?" she asked, afraid to even consider that he might be apologizing for being such a royal ass. But as she met his gaze, she realized there was real contrition staring back at her and she couldn't help but soften just a little. "You're sorry. That's a start," she admitted, glancing away. She didn't trust herself while he continued to look at her that way. "Sorry for what?"

He mopped away the water dripping from his face with a paper towel and threw it away before answering. "I'm sorry for a lot of things," he conceded, surprising her. "But I'm mostly sorry for the things I said this morning. I was out of line."

"Yes, you were," she agreed, lifting her chin against the aggrieved look he sent her. She wasn't going to make it easy for him. He deserved to squirm a bit. "Go on."

He cocked his head to the side. "You want to come and sit down so we can talk it over?"

She hoisted Jenna on her hip. "Not really. What I'd like to do is walk out that front door and forget I ever had any feelings for you."

His expression darkened for a moment and she sensed she'd hit a very raw nerve. It was mean of her to poke like that but she was still raw herself. Feeling the ghost of her mother chiding her from beyond the grave, she gritted her teeth and counted to ten so she could talk without wanting to scream at him…or worse, just break down and cry some more.

"Fair enough," he said, sighing even as he looked away for a moment. "Listen, I just want to say I had no right to jump all over you like that. I don't know what came over me…I just reacted and I'm really ashamed of my behavior."

That was something. And she believed him. One thing Archer had never been, and she didn't think he'd change colors overnight, was a liar. His admission went a long way toward thawing the ice she felt creeping up around her heart. But even though he

apologized, the words were still there hanging between them and Marissa didn't know how to dispel
their lingering poison.

"Did you mean what you said about…just wanting to relive old times?" she asked, hating that her
voice came out sounding small and pathetic, but
truly, it's how she felt because his answer meant so
much to her.

He appeared conflicted and the insides of her
stomach dropped. She almost didn't want to hear his
answer. If he said yes, it would destroy what she'd
thought was happening between them; if he said no,
it would make her want something that had already
been proven to fail. It was a lose-lose situation for
them both. Why the hell did she ask such a dumb
question?

He came toward her and she was tempted to bolt
but her feet remained rooted. Jenna looked up at
Archer and grinned, grabbing at his face with a
chubby hand and suddenly leaning out of Marissa's
arms toward him.

Archer's expression surely mirrored her own as
Jenna went happily into his arms. She gurgled and
in her own language said quite a lot but to them it
only sounded like adorable gibberish. Marissa looked
at Archer and shook her head, confused as he was.
"She's never that open with people," Marissa said. "I
mean, she screamed any time Ruben ever got near
her and she's just not the kind of baby who willingly

goes to strangers. Here, I'll take her," she offered but as Marissa reached for Jenna, the baby twisted away and held on to Archer.

"Jenna?" Marissa stared, frowning. "What's wrong?"

Archer held the baby, at first as if she were going to morph into something dangerous, then as she babbled, looking up at him with those beautifully dark eyes, he softened and Marissa hitched in a painfully tight breath. She'd never seen him around children, not like this. Jenna fit in his arms as though she was his own. "She's fine," he said, moving to the sofa to sit. He held her as if she were fine china, full of wonder at the softness of her skin and the silky hair that fell from her head in a black cloud. He glanced at Marissa. "You know...I never realized how much she looks like you," he said, settling Jenna against his chest, where she remained, completely content, even giving Marissa a drooly grin as if to say, *Stop worrying,* Tía.

"Well, Mercedes and I looked a lot alike," Marissa conceded, yet her heart warmed that Archer would notice.

Archer shook his head. "I never thought you and your sister looked a thing alike."

"Oh?"

"Nope. No offense but your sister had a hard edge to her that distracted from her good looks. When she looked at you, I got the feeling she was sizing you up into two classes that basically answered one question—What can you do for me? You never had that look."

"She wasn't always like that," Marissa murmured, fighting against the ache that she knew was just grief in another form. But Archer was right. Mercedes had changed into someone who was exactly like that. Except toward the end. Marissa liked to think if she hadn't died...

"When we were growing up, she was the one who was always looking out for me," Marissa said, propping her head on her crooked elbow against the sofa cushion, willing to share a few good memories of her sister if only to deflect away from the conversation they should've been finishing. "You know we grew up on the bad side of Oakland. There were a lot of gangs and staying out of trouble was harder than you'd think. I was picked on, bullied, beat up a few times, Mercedes always had my back. And it wasn't easy for her. She took a couple hits that probably should've been mine but she never complained. Never said a word."

"What about your mom?"

"She did what she could but she worked two jobs to keep a roof over our heads. She counted on the fact that we'd take care of each other. She wasn't there to help with homework, sign permission slips, or pack lunches. Mercedes did that for me."

"Who did it for Mercedes?" he asked.

Marissa shook her head. "No one. I wonder some-times if her life would've turned out different if she hadn't had to spend all her time and energy on me. That's why I couldn't turn my back on her when things started to get bad with Ruben. She'd given me so much, helped me get to college and start a new life that didn't begin in that place we grew up. I couldn't just walk away."

"I understand why you felt obligated," he said but she quickly corrected him.

"No. It wasn't obligation. It was love. I loved her so much for giving me a chance to succeed. I wanted to be there for her like she was for me. But she started to change. The lifestyle made her different. And you know the rest."

He digested the information silently, then said, "You're a good person. And I'm really sorry for saying what I said earlier. Can you forgive me?"

Of course she could. She probably already had but she wondered where they went from here. She hadn't realized how much she missed him until she saw him again. That yearning flared alive quick and bright, hot and dangerous. And now there was this mess with Ruben. And the fact that she'd stolen a child and, Lord help her, possibly killed a man. Their ob-stacles went way beyond her penchant for stability. In the face of these new problems, her reasons for pushing him away three years ago seemed like child's play.

"Did I say something wrong?" he asked, concern pulling at his brows. Jenna swiveled her little head to stare at Marissa, too.

"No. You said everything right," she murmured, shaking her head. "I...I don't know. I just think my head is a mess right now. I should tell you what I was going to tell you when this whole argument started."

"Okay."

She drew a deep breath. "I don't regret last night. At first I thought I did but after I got over my initial reaction I realized I didn't regret it at all. What upset me was the realization that I threw away our relationship and there was no going back. Not even if I wanted to," she said, looking up quickly to gauge his reaction.

"Are you saying you want to try again?" he asked carefully.

"I'm saying I wish that we could but now it's impossible."

"Why?"

"Because I would never want to start a relationship under these circumstances. Even if we didn't have a mountain of baggage from the past, there's all this new garbage to deal with and when I say garbage I don't think I need to remind you that I'm talking about a drug lord whose baby I stole. I'm most definitely facing kidnapping charges, not to mention first-degree murder if this all goes south. I wouldn't want to drag you through that with me. I won't have your life trashed because mine is."

"Why do women say one thing and mean another?" he asked, startling her with his question.

"You lost me."

"And you lost me about ten minutes ago. All I heard was you want to get back together but you don't want to get back together because we have baggage and your life is a mess."

"Yeah…what's confusing about that?"

"Everything, woman," he said, further shocking her with a grin. He switched Jenna to his other knee and then leaned in and pulled Marissa to him in one motion. Then he planted his lips against hers in a move that sent warm tingles dancing down to her toes. "You're stuck with me for the time being so just stop worrying about the stuff that we can't do a thing about," he said against her lips, tickling the soft flesh there. He pulled away and she missed the contact already. "First things first. We figure out how to keep your pretty ass out of prison for taking off with this little princess. Second, we deal with our baggage. But, don't worry, we've got our hands too full with the first task to get into the second right away, so chill."

"Chill?"

"Yeah."

"Have you ever known me to do that?"

He didn't even need to give it thought. "Nope. But I know you're a quick study. You'll figure it out."

She laughed and a weight lifted from her chest that she hadn't realized she'd been carrying around. It wasn't a solution exactly, but it was a start. And at least she didn't have to leave, which was a good thing. She had nowhere else to go.

"Listen, I have an idea," he said, surprising her into a wary smile from the warmth shining from his eyes. She'd gladly spend a lifetime basking in the light of that heat if he'd let her, she mused with a private sigh of longing and desire that felt good to acknowledge. When Archer realized she was waiting for him to continue, he said, "I say we take Josh's offer up on the barbecue and pretend like we're both normal for an evening." She started to protest at his implication but he silenced her with a quick kiss that took her breath away in spite of its brevity in order to continue, "We'll drink a beer, eat hamburgers and hot dogs and Mary's potato salad. We'll listen to Mary's gossip and secretly be grateful that we're on Mary's good side and we'll just enjoy…being normal. It'll be a nice change of scenery."

"I'm normal," she muttered, frowning.

"You're far from normal," he disagreed amiably. "But that's okay. You're in pretty good company."

At that she smiled but it faded as she considered the situation she was in. "Josh is bound to ask questions. What will we say? I'm a terrible liar," she said, worrying her bottom lip as she thought of her unfortunate tendency to fidget when she lied.

"He won't," Archer assured her, his grin telling her he agreed with her admission. "I've already given him the CliffsNotes. Beyond that he won't ask unless you feel up to sharing. Josh is good that way."

She looked up at him and lost herself for a moment in the depth of his eyes and the well of concern she saw there. Drawing a deep breath she offered a tentative smile. "Okay," she said, and then with more conviction as she warmed to the idea, added, "You know…you might be right. A barbecue with friends might be wonderful. Let's do it."

"Good. You and the baby go get ready while I call Josh."

CHAPTER NINE

JOSH MET THEM AT THE door of his parents' house with an offering of a beer for Archer, which he accepted with a grateful nod. Archer was about to run the gauntlet known as Mary Halvorsen and he'd need a little something to keep him from cowering like a whipped dog.

He didn't have long to wait, either. Mary appeared from the kitchen, a thunderous expression on her face, wielding a spatula in her hand as if it was a whipping stick, and Archer knew he was about to get his ass chewed. The sick thing? He was totally looking forward to it.

"Archer Brant, I've half a mind to kick your sorry behind out of my house for abandoning your family during your little pity-party instead of taking your licks like a man. Disappearing like that! Not one word of where you were or what you were doing…I worried myself sick to death wondering if you were lying in a ditch somewhere dying or worse. I didn't feed and clothe you, and go toe-to-toe with that fool-headed principal for constantly trying to expel you your senior year just for you to repay my hard work and loving attention tossing it away like that. You hear me, boy? I won't stand for it. Manners don't lose their place just because you're too big to whup." She pointed her spatula at him with a narrowed stare and added, "What have you got to say for yourself?"

He smothered a grin because for all her mean-eyed lecturing, he knew she was happy to see him and it was the knowledge that he meant something to this family that sobered him appropriately. "I've missed you, too, Mrs. H.," he said. "No one makes potato salad like you. And that's the God's honest truth. Can you forgive me for being an idiot?"

"Of course I can," she said, breaking into a wide grin before gathering him into her arms, pressing him against her large bosom as if she'd given birth to him, same as her three boys. "This town hasn't been the same without you, dear. My boys have gone and become respectable, you know. Now there's no one to keep the deputies busy," she said playfully as she pulled away. It was then that she noticed Marissa and Jenna waiting behind him. She gave him a healthy pat on the cheek and then pushed him out of the way, gesturing with a warning. "Stay out of that potato salad until it's time to eat. Now, who do we have here? You must be Marissa, Archer's former fiancée." Marissa startled and her gaze flew to Archer, but before he could interject, Mary had hustled Marissa toward the kitchen with a delighted expression that Archer realized too late signaled trouble. Marissa had been worried about the wrong Halvorsen doing the digging.

Josh laughed and pulled a reluctant Archer toward the porch where everyone else was gathered, saying, "Sorry, bud. Mom's got her now. You should've known better."

Archer chuckled. Yeah…he should've.

MARISSA DIDN'T KNOW what to think of this buxom, stout woman but there was something about her that she liked, even if she was a little wary.

"I love a good story," Mary said, grabbing a box of Bisquick and shaking out a healthy portion for what Marissa assumed would be a fresh batch of biscuits. "I suspect yours is worth telling," she surmised with a knowing smile. "Of course, you don't have to share if you're not comfortable but I hate a mystery and I'm bound to find out anyway so fair warning."

"What makes you think I have a good story?" Marissa hedged, shifting Jenna on her hip, watching as Mary pounded the dough and then rolled it out with an efficiency that spoke of years of practice.

"The bruise for one. And I know Archer didn't give it to you because he's not that kind of man. I practically raised him, you know."

"Yes, Archer mentioned you were very kind to

him," she murmured. "And you're right. Archer would never hit a woman."

Mary punched perfectly round biscuits from the dough. "See? I knew your story was one worth listening to. Start at the beginning, dear. And don't leave anything out."

At first Marissa didn't have any inclination to share the sordid details of the past seventy-two hours but there was something oddly cathartic and soothing about sharing her burden with Mary Halvorsen. She left out the part where she sold her dignity to Ruben for her niece but Marissa could tell by the quiet contemplation on Mary's face that the older woman knew she was sanitizing certain details and it was okay.

"So even though he has no reason to care, Archer has taken us in for the time being," Marissa concluded, drawing a deep breath as she finished. She waited for Mary's response but Mary took the time to attend to her biscuits as if she needed a moment to digest everything Marissa had shared, and Marissa felt a frisson of worry that she'd made a mistake.

Mary pulled the biscuits, golden brown, from the oven and paused to take an appreciative sniff before placing them on the counter to cool. She replaced her oven mitt on the hook by the stove and then faced Marissa with the fiercest look in her eyes.

"That man you're running from deserves to have his testicles sheared off and fried," she said, shaking her head. "Some people are just born bad. I'm sorry you're caught up in all this. You seem like a good person. I'm not sure what we can offer you right now aside from support and a hot meal but I hope this situation works itself out and you can put it all behind you."

Marissa's eyes watered. "Thank you. Me, too."

Laughter drifted in from outside as the guys traded jokes, stories, or whatever else that men do when they're left to their own devices and Mary smiled brightly, effectively ending the somber tone of the previous conversation, by announcing, "Time to eat!"

And suddenly, Marissa was starved and couldn't agree more.

IT WAS LATE BY THE time they returned to Archer's place and fatigue pulled at Marissa's eyelids. She'd spent the evening listening to Josh and Mary recount tales of Archer's penchant for trouble and laughed as Archer's cheeks reddened a little bit more with each story. She found it highly ironic that he went into the military when he obviously had had such issues with authority as a kid. She'd chatted with Josh's wife, Tasha, about seemingly suburban topics such as kids, jobs and current movies playing in theaters and it was wonderful.

Archer had been right. Doing something that smacked of normal had provided relief from the tension and fear that kept her insides tied in a knot and she was sorry to see it end.

Marissa tucked Jenna into bed and then after washing her face and changing, she found herself outside Archer's door. She placed her hand on the wood, hesitant to knock yet not quite willing to end the night just yet.

What was she saying by standing there? She closed her eyes briefly, knowing full well what it said and her heart rate tripped a beat. She knocked softly.

The door opened and Archer stood there, his eyes registering the same desire blotting out the sensible side of her and she went into his arms wordlessly.

ARCHER KISSED HER SLOW and deep, pouring everything he felt for her into the tender touch of his lips against hers. She was like a drug coursing through his veins, demanding everything he had and more but he gladly surrendered, losing himself in the heat they created.

It was dangerous to pretend, a voice whispered, but he silenced it ruthlessly. He needed her, had never stopped, and he was going to enjoy every moment until circumstances dictated otherwise.

Sliding his hands reverently down her body, he thrilled at her little gasps and moans against his mouth, and then led her to the bed.

"Archer," she whispered, a slight frown pulling on

her brows but he shushed her with another kiss, not willing to let reality intrude on their time together.

"No talking," he murmured and she nodded her assent before he removed her nightshirt, baring her breasts to his fevered gaze. "So perfect, so beautiful…"

She smiled sweetly, reaching her arms to curl around his neck, drawing him to her. "You said no talking," she reminded him in a husky whisper as the silky friction of her thighs rubbed against his painfully hard erection, and then she opened to him, ready and eager.

He wanted to tell her he loved her. Wanted to start over. Wanted the life they would've had if they hadn't walked away. Wanted her in his bed every night and beside him every morning. Wanted so much. Wanted…everything.

Impossible, the voice whispered. He squeezed his eyes shut and tightened his hold on her, as though afraid she might disappear if he let go. She sensed the change in him and he felt her fingertips flutter across his temple to frame his face. "Archer…" Her soft voice pulled at him, forcing him to meet her gaze in the moonlit darkness. "Make love to me as if we don't have tomorrow," she said, right as a tear escaped and slid down her cheek. He wiped it away and knew they were sharing the same thought.

Because tomorrow was not promised to anyone. Least of all those walking toward a cliff.

CHAPTER TEN

ARCHER'S CELL PHONE buzzed to life on his desk and he grabbed it before it vibrated right onto the floor.

It was Rico.

"What you got for me?" he asked, flexing his shoulder as he cradled the cell to his ear on the opposite side. Damn, he really shouldn't have pushed it that hard. The doc was probably going to bury his ass in paperwork so deep he'd need an infrared camera to find it again. "Tell me you've got a lead."

"I wouldn't exactly call it a lead but I wouldn't hesitate to call it a glimmer of hope in your tragic little scenario."

"Great," he said wryly. "Spill it."

"Okay, seems this punk Ruben has a juvenile record. Whistle-clean as an adult, probably figured out how to get others to do his dirty work by then, but as a snot-nosed kid he was quite a little thug."

Archer wasn't going to waste time asking Rico how he got access to files that were sealed; he simply wanted the details. "Go on. Violent crime? Drugs?

Anything we could use to tie him to anything recent?" he asked.

"What self-respecting little gangbanger wouldn't have a few drug and assault charges on his rap sheet," Rico laughed. Archer heard the tapping of a pencil and the squeak of Rico's office chair as he swiveled to no doubt read the computer screen he was wired into. "So, seems young Ruben Antonio Ortiz was a mean son of a bitch. Not your run-of-the-mill stuff. The kid was kind of sadistic. Some animal cruelty charges that stand out. Appears the kid doused a stray pitbull with gasoline and lit the poor sucker on fire just to watch it burn. Sick, man."

"Maybe he was training to be a serial killer," Archer surmised lightly but inside he was turning over the information slowly and deliberately and not liking what he was seeing. This was the guy who was Jenna's father? He shuddered at the idea of him getting anywhere near the baby girl. "Anything else?" he asked.

"Oh, shit, gobs. It's a miracle the kid didn't do serious time. I mean he did stints in juvie but nothing that would stick to him. More's the pity, I say. This guy is one class act. You want me to e-mail over the file?"

"Yeah. I could use a little light reading."

"I thought so." There was a beat between them, then Rico said, "What's the story with the woman?

She Ruben's girl or something? Get smacked around and then came to you for help?"

"Not hardly. If you knew Marissa you'd never guess that. She's not his type."

"But she's yours?"

"I don't have a type," he said, except that wasn't true. His type had melt-me brown eyes and a wicked pair of lips who just happened to be in the living room playing with the baby. He smiled. "Hey, I owe you, man. This is solid info. Hit me back if you find anything else."

"Will do." The camaraderie in Rico's voice made his chest feel tight. Before signing off Rico said, "Hey, man, you want some backup? I have a few vacay days I could cash in, come up and see this cabin you're always bragging about. I could use the fresh air, I think."

"Just quit smoking and you'll have all the fresh air you need," Archer said, then added, "Thanks but no thanks. I got it covered. But I know where to find you if I do."

"You got it, Arch. Be safe, man."

"I'll do my best."

A minute later Archer's e-mail program dinged signaling an incoming file. He opened the message and downloaded. Moments later the zipped file opened and he scanned young Ortiz's criminal record.

Light reading, indeed. Archer knew dirtbags. He'd

put a few away, killed a handful more, and watched as more than he cared to count walked away on a technicality thanks to the screwed up nature of the justice system. But as he read Ortiz's file, he saw more than your average street-rat hood. He saw cunning, ambition, and the one quality that always set him on edge, instability. Ortiz was capable of anything—murder was likely something he didn't even lose sleep over—and he also saw that he didn't quit until he got what he wanted. The question was... How badly did Ortiz want his child...or for that matter, Marissa? The answer didn't matter. The man was dangerous and just knowing that he might be looking for them made Archer want to get them far away.

MARISSA PUT JENNA DOWN for her afternoon nap and, for want of something to do, wandered back downstairs. There was really no help for it. She was bored stiff.

And really, what did she expect? They were holed up in a house with no end in sight. The barbecue at the Halvorsens' had just made it so much more clear that this was no way to live. She was accustomed to regular exercise, both mental and physical, and a full wardrobe, for crying out loud. It was hard not to feel a bit stir-crazy in this environment.

Even if the cabin was lovely in a modern rustic sort of way with its walls made from white birch planks, framed by giant windows and high ceilings. Sure, the place was gorgeous and spacious and all the things she would've loved if it were their house and she were puttering around in the garden and there wasn't a mad-case nut-job hunting her down. She sighed. If only.

There were too many "if onlys" going around in her head to continue along that vein unless she wanted to continually depress herself. None represented her reality aside from the part where she'd neatly imprisoned herself in a very nice cage.

"You've got that look in your eyes," Archer observed, coming into the room from his study.

She turned away. "And what look would that be?"

"The look that says you want to rearrange furniture or spring clean."

She scoffed. "I've never had such a look."

His raised eyebrow indicated he disagreed. "You do too. It's been a while but I recognize it just the same. And the answer is no. You can't rearrange my furniture. I like it just the way it is."

She glared at him. So she wasn't the type to suffer a cluttered house—was that a crime? She dismissed him with a wave. "Don't worry. I have no intentions of moving your precious furniture…even if the sofa is placed entirely wrong."

"All right. I'll bite. What's wrong with the sofa?"

She glanced back at the sofa and then back at him. "Well, if it were me, I'd put the sofa over here, away from the wall, and facing the morning window. You've a gorgeous view that's going to waste. You're a morning person so you should be able to drink your coffee and watch the sunrise from this wide beautiful window," she said, cocking her head to the side, envisioning the change. "Yes. That would be much better than the way you have it now. But that's if it were me, which it's not so it's moot."

"Yep."

Man of many words. She gave a quick, annoyed roll of her eyes, still edgy and still wanting to run the hell out of there and back to her life. If only there weren't a psycho murderer just waiting for her to try. She didn't want to think of Ruben. Even allowing his name into her mental theater made her want to cringe and hyperventilate. "Don't you have any checkers or something?" she blurted, hating the high-pitched, irritated tone of her voice. She sounded like a shrew.

"Checkers?" he repeated. "You mean the game?"

"Of course I mean the game. What other kind of checkers is there?" Her annoyance sharpened her voice.

"No."

"Of course you don't," she muttered, sinking into the sofa with a groan. "I'm going to lose my mind one brain cell at a time locked away in this house."

"You're bored."

"Hell yes, I'm bored. I'm so bored I'm half

tempted to return to my apartment just so I can clean up the mess Ruben's thugs left behind!"

His sharp stare moved to hers, taking in her last statement with something akin to concern. "How do you know your apartment is trashed? I thought you said you ran straight from Ruben's compound to here."

She waved away his alarm. "I called my boss to let her know that I was okay. She was worried—"

He moved so quickly she barely had time to gasp. "When did you call?"

She frowned. What was the problem? "I called a couple days ago. It was no big deal. Honestly, what's wrong? You're scaring me."

His voice was calm but his eyes told a different story, and suddenly she was very scared for Layla. "Why do you have that look on your face?" she asked, a bit fearful. Her gut clenched and quivered before he even answered.

"I think you just put your friend in danger."

She drew a sharp breath then let it out in a painful whoosh. "Oh, God…how?"

"Ruben isn't going to go through regular channels to get his kid back. He can't exactly go to the cops, even though he has a few on the take, because it will raise suspicion, start fueling questions that he doesn't want answered. So he's going to go old-school. And since you have no remaining family to go squeeze, he's going to start going to friends…coworkers."

She shook her head even though what Archer said rang true. "Layla's a scientist...white collar... grew up with a white-picket-fence upbringing...she wouldn't recognize danger unless it was disguised as a microbe under a microscope." The tightening in her gut worsened and she thought she might be sick. "Oh, God...what if Ruben does something terrible to Layla? You don't know what he's capable of...sick, twisted, cruel...oh, no...."

His mouth formed a grim line but he stilled her with a firm hand on hers. "Then he's going to find more than he bargained for," Archer promised, but even that dark vow didn't stop her stomach from roiling. Everyone she loved...she couldn't fathom losing Archer, too.

It was just too much.

ARCHER EYED THE WINDOWS, wide and welcoming at their best, but sporting weak spots and highly accessible at their worst, and started shuttering the house.

"What are you doing?" she asked, her voice strained. "Can I help?"

"No, stay away from the windows. I'm making it that much harder for someone to see inside the house. Stay where you are and don't go outside."

He caught her shivering and he paused for only a moment to reassure her. "I'm just taking precautions. But the more I learn about Ruben Ortiz, the less I'm interested in taking chances. Can you remember whether or not you told your boss where you were?"

"Her name is Layla," she answered numbly but then shook her head. "I just said I needed some personal time. Because of my sister."

"Let me see your phone," he demanded. "I need to see what kind of system you're on and if you have GPS," he said when she frowned.

She moved to her purse and pulled her cell phone out to hand it to him.

He cracked open the back, his mouth tightening. "I was hoping it was one of the older models…but it's not. State of the art. And it's fully equipped with GPS."

"So? Isn't that a good thing?"

"Under normal circumstances I'd say yes. But we're not dealing with normal. You might as well have tagged a homing device on your ass. If Ruben were smart, and he had the right contacts, all it would take to find you is to track your location using your phone."

She gasped and stared, unable to believe she'd been so naive. Suddenly having a phone with so many cool features, like wireless Internet and salsa ringtones, didn't seem so great. "What do I do with it?" she asked, still staring at her phone as if it had morphed into a scorpion and was heading straight for her.

"Well, for starters…" He busted open the phone,

causing her to jump, and then ripped its poor guts out. "The chip is what makes it work. So, we make it stop working."

She looked at the destruction of her very expensive and now useless phone and wanted to cry. "Do you think that will be covered by the warranty?" she asked in a whisper and suddenly Archer realized she wasn't talking about the phone any longer. Her knees buckled and she collapsed on the sofa, a quivering pile of nerves, circling the edge of a breakdown. She put her head in her hands and great big sobs started rolling out of her.

"Hey, what's this?" Archer asked, pulling her into his arms. Her sobs just got louder. She was beyond the place where rational, coherent thinking lived. He must've sensed this for his arms simply tightened and he made soft soothing noises that were so unlike Archer she was certain she'd fallen into the arms of someone else. "Everything's going to be all right," he promised, prompting her to pull away.

"How do you know that?" she asked, wiping at her nose with the back of her hand. "You don't. Ruben is a killer. You don't know what kind of man he is and I've brought him to you. I don't know what to do anymore. I'm out of ideas…I don't even know what I was thinking when I showed up at your doorstep!"

He gently grasped her face in his palms and held her stare as he said, "You did the right thing. I'm here for you. Ruben will have to come through me before he can ever get to you and that's a promise."

Her eyes watered anew and she wondered why Archer was being so good to her when she'd done nothing to deserve it. "You don't know him," she whispered, wanting desperately to hit a do-over button and rethink the whole situation.

He wiped the trail of moisture from her cheek with the pad of his thumb. "I'll find a way to get you through this. There's a solution. We will find it."

She hiccupped softly, so wanting to believe him, yet fear rode her hard. She would never forgive herself if Archer ended up caught in the cross fire. "He's obsessed with me," she admitted in a hushed tone, hating even saying it aloud. "He won't quit."

Archer's voice took on a mean quality that alternately scared the life out of her and sent a dark thrill down her back as he said, "He will when I put a bullet in his brain."

ARCHER HADN'T MEANT TO reveal the intense twist of his thoughts but holding Marissa's shaking body had done a number on his self-control. Needing to put some distance between them so he could get his head on straight, he gently pushed her away. Her subtle, wounded frown said it all but he didn't have the luxury of letting his messed-up heart get in the way of protecting her. From now on, she was his assignment to protect. Thus far, he'd been pretty damn lax and that was his mistake. It was a miracle neither one of them had eaten a bullet by now.

"Listen, we're no longer safe here," he said sternly, ignoring her look of distress. "We need to get someplace that hasn't been compromised."

"But we don't know if Ruben knows to use the GPS in the phone...I mean, he's street-smart but he doesn't have beyond a high school education, if that. Maybe we don't need to leave," she protested, the note of desperation clear in her voice. "I don't want to leave. I feel safe here."

He shook his head. "This is not an easily defensible place. I won't take further chances with your life. I want you to go upstairs and pack only what you absolutely need."

"Yes, because I came with so much," she retorted bitterly, her voice still watery but some of her former spirit returning. "What I have could fit in a backpack."

"Good. Same goes for the baby."

"She needs her diapers, bottles...her toys..." Her voice trailed as he shook his head at the toys, and tears filled her eyes again. He knew this was hard. She tightened her mouth with a short jerk of her head. "Fine. No toys."

"Someday when this is all over, she won't remember that she went without a few rattles and stuffed animals when she was a baby," he said, trying to make Marissa feel better but it wasn't having the desired effect.

"Someday when this is all over? It might never be over."

He caught the indescribably sad expression on her face and it made him want to promise her the moon if only to never see such hopelessness again, but he couldn't make promises about a tomorrow that may not come for any of them. He could only do his best.

A violent chill passed through him as Kandy's dead face floated into his memory.

Sometimes his best wasn't good enough.

CHAPTER ELEVEN

MARISSA STARED MOROSELY at her bag, almost numb to the situation. She had no idea where they were going. Archer hadn't been forthcoming with a lot of details, and she felt wildly out of control of her own life.

Archer appeared from upstairs, carrying a black bag of his own as he came downstairs. She took note of his appearance. If there was a word to describe him it would be *lethal*. He had a gun—she couldn't really say what make or model because honestly, they all looked big, black and scary to her mind—tucked into his waistband and when he lifted his pant leg to adjust the strap encircling his calf she saw an evil-looking knife with a wicked serrated edge strapped in a leather holster attached there.

Holy Mother Mary, were they going to South America?

"Is this really necessary?" she asked, eyeing the weapons of destruction that he wore with ease. She added with growing discomfort, "I mean, you look like you're going to war or something."

"Tools of the trade," he answered, bending down to double-check the contents of his bag. He looked up and asked, "You all ready to go?"

"Where are we going?" she countered, picking Jenna from the floor at her feet to hoist her onto her hip. She wiped at a line of drool and rubbed it off on her jeans. "I just think we should think this through before we make hasty decisions."

He ignored her. "I take that as a yes. Good. We'll take my Cherokee. I'm assuming the baby has a car seat of some sort?"

"Of course she does," Marissa said, irritated. "It's in my car. I'll go get it."

He stopped her with a hand gesture. "You stay put. I'll get it."

She made a noise of exasperation. "Aren't you going just a little too far? My car is parked in back."

He took a step toward her, his expression one of business and stern purpose. She was tempted to take a faltering step back but she held her ground. She was tired of being intimidated even if Archer thought he was doing it for her own good. She gave him a glare to communicate that fact. It didn't seem to faze him. He said, "Your safety has been compromised. We're going somewhere safe. I've already called in a favor. We don't know just how far Ortiz is willing to go to get what he wants and I'm not going to take the chance. If you're ready…let's hit the road."

Marissa swallowed the retort on her tongue. He

was doing this to protect her—that's what she needed to keep front and center in her mind but she was already tired of running. What a terrible criminal she made. Life on the run wasn't all it was cracked up to be, she thought with dark humor.

ARCHER HATED THAT HE had to do this but he didn't see any other way.

"So where are we going?" she asked as they climbed into his Cherokee, showing only mild distress at the dark stains marring the worn cloth seats as she slid into the front, the baby secure in her car seat behind her. "Is it far?"

He cast a quick look her way before answering. "It's probably about a forty-five minute drive."

Her expression twisted into something quizzical as she said, "That's not far at all. Where is this place? Yosemite or Fresno?"

"Technically, Yosemite. But we're not going to be near the valley floor. It's a small winter cabin up in Wawona, owned by Josh's family. He said we could use it to hole up for a few days until I can get a handle on how to catch Ortiz."

"We're going from your cabin in the woods to another cabin in the woods?" she asked incredulously. "How is that safer than just staying here?"

"I told you, this place is compromised. If I had my choices I'd rather take you to a safe house owned by the Bureau but I don't think we're ready to go there. Not yet. So, until then, Josh's place will have to do."

She looked away, sullen. "I'd rather stay here."

"Yeah, well, I'd rather not take the chance that Ruben is smarter than we thought and we wake up with our jugulars split wide-open."

"I doubt he even knows what GPS is," she maintained stubbornly. "How about we just stay with Josh and Tasha for the night? I'm sure they'd let us crash on their sofa."

"Never underestimate your enemy," he warned, thinking of Vincent and how he'd done exactly that because the guy had been a low-level street-rat hood who barely held an eighth grade education. Didn't take a genius to pick a lock and pull the trigger. "And I know you don't mean that about Josh and Tasha. You don't want them involved with this any more than I do."

"I know," she said with an unhappy sigh. "I'm sorry. I shouldn't have said that. You're right. I wouldn't dare bring any trouble on their heads. I'm not thinking straight right now," she said, her fingers going to rub her temple as if trying to assuage a pulsing pain there.

He understood her desperation and didn't fault her. "Don't worry. It's not permanent. A night or two. I just don't feel comfortable here until we get some more details. I want eyes on Ruben and until I do…he's a wild card that I'm not willing to gamble on."

Her defeated sigh did wonders for his self-esteem as she said, "It will take longer than a few days. The man is like the wind. Nothing stands in his way and he goes wherever he wants."

"All the more reason to proceed with caution."

She finally gave a short nod but she was clearly still unhappy about it. He didn't blame her. He wasn't crazy about leaving, either, but he wasn't about to take foolish chances with their lives.

"Have a little faith," he said, to which she simply looked away to stare out the window. *"Rissa,"* he said her name softly and she turned reluctantly. Once he had her gaze, he made her a promise. "I'm not going to let anything happen to you or Jenna. You have my word."

She swallowed and her eyes watered a little but she nodded. "Thanks."

"But?" He sensed there was something she wasn't saying.

Marissa returned to the window. "Just drive. If we're going to get going, we ought to do it before it gets dark. Jenna doesn't travel all that well for long distances."

Dissatisfied, but agreeing with her logic, he put the car in Drive and headed out. Josh, God love the man, didn't even hesitate when Archer had asked for permission to use the cabin. He'd simply told him where the key was hidden. When this was all over, Archer owed him. Big-time.

Connecting to Rico through his Bluetooth Jawbone, he gave him the quick and dirty of the situation.

"Smart call," Rico said when he'd finished. "You destroy the chip?"

"Yes. It's in pieces and it ain't coming back."

"Good. Where you heading?"

"Friend has a family cabin up in the high country. Service is sketchy but no worse than what I've got at my place. When I get there I'll give you the home number in case the cell craps out. In the meantime, I want you to do some snooping around as to why there was no assault charges filed against Ortiz when he smacked Marissa's sister around. There's gotta be a paper trail somewhere, even if someone tried to bury it."

"You know, I do have a job, unlike some people who are enjoying a life of leisure with a beautiful woman," Rico teased.

"How do you know she's beautiful?" Archer asked, his hackles rising along with his sudden suspicion. "You've never met."

"No, but I'm a whiz when it comes to hacking. Not that I needed my skills since I just checked out her driver's license, courtesy of the DMV. Hot little *mamacita* you've got there. I wouldn't mind spending a little R & R in the mountains with a sweet tart like that."

"Watch your mouth, Rico, before I zip it shut for you."

"Testy. And rude. That's what you are, you know that?"

"So I've been told. Can you do it or not?"

"You know I can. Hit me back with that number when you get there so I can triangulate your position in case you need backup."

"No one knows about this cabin in Ruben's circles. We should be fine but just to err on the side of safety...yeah, sounds like a solid plan."

Archer clicked off and caught Marissa's curiosity. "Teammate of mine. He's a solid guy. We can trust him," he assured her.

"Are you friends?" she asked.

Friends? He wouldn't call Rico a friend, would he? He had to think about it for a minute. Finally, he shrugged. "We don't golf together or anything but he's a good guy," he answered.

"I didn't know you golf."

"I don't." Her chuckle made him grin. "What?"

She simply shook her head. "Nothing. So tell me more about this cabin. Does it have running water?"

"Yes. But no dishwasher. And it's a vacation rental during the summer, so we'll have to wash the sheets and leave it as we found it for the next person."

"How many times have you been there?"

"Well, when Josh and me were teens we used to come up here when it was empty and hang out."

"Ah, so you used to go there to party."

He laughed. "Yeah. But it was cool as long as we didn't mess the place up. We did some pretty stupid things but nothing that ever got out of hand. It's a good place. I think you'll like it."

"Hmm," was all she said before she returned her gaze out the window. He knew this was hard for her. It wasn't like they were running off for a relaxing vacation. The threat was there and it sat between them, dark and menacing, squatting on whatever good feelings that threatened to bloom between them. It sucked. He wished he were taking them to a beautiful five-star resort with room service, all the amenities, near a white-sand beach with plenty of sunshine. He wasn't knocking Josh's family cabin—he had a lot of great memories in that place—but let's face it, he knew it wasn't much to look at. And right now was not the best time to visit. There was likely still snow on the ground, which meant the pipes might be frozen, and the only source of heat in the entire house was an old floor heater that you had to practically stand over to get the benefit of any warmth. No, it wasn't the Hilton, but it was isolated, no one in Ruben's circles would be able to find it, and his main job was to keep Marissa and Jenna safe.

Later, he promised himself, he would take Marissa somewhere beautiful where she could be pampered like she deserved.

MARISSA WAS DOING HER best to keep up a brave front but inside she quivered and shook. Her nerves were shot. She wasn't cut out for this kind of thing. She missed her ordinary life, even if it was a bit on the boring side. Right about now, she'd give anything to slide back into that staid, predictable routine of going to work, taking care of Jenna, grocery shopping and diaper detail with the knowledge that she'd do everything all over again the next day. It was hard to imagine that every now and again she'd chaffed at that ordinary life.

"Tell me about your work," Archer said, breaking into her thoughts. She didn't want to think about her work and the possibility that she'd never return to what she'd been working on. She shrugged and then shook her head. Archer seemed to understand. "It's okay. We don't have to talk if you don't want to," he said.

"Thanks," she murmured, returning to the scenery. She thought of her mother, dead for the past nine years and wondered if she'd watched Mercedes die. Marissa blinked back tears. She hoped if Mama was there, she had guided Mercedes to heaven. She hated to think that her sister died alone and afraid.

"Do you think Mercedes suffered?" she asked in a small voice.

There was hesitation in Archer's tone as he answered. "From what you've told me it was a gun-

shot wound to the head…and usually that's a pretty
fast way to die, unless…"

"Unless what?"

"Unless the bullet ricocheted off the skull and
banged around the brain—" he stopped and Marissa
was intensely grateful. She'd been foolish to ask.
The details weren't likely to make her feel better and
Archer must've realized this. "I'm sure it was quick,"
he finished.

Whether that was true or not, Marissa didn't want
to know. She'd just needed to hear it.

"Mercedes was such a force of nature, it's hard to
believe she's gone."

"She'll always live on in your heart and in Jenna,"
Archer offered, trying to be helpful. She supposed it
was true but she wanted her sister back, in the flesh,
not by proxy. "Tell me a story about Mercedes, something you remember that makes you feel good," he
suggested.

She appreciated his trying to make her feel better
but she was mired in grief—not only for her sister but
for herself—and she wasn't sure she had the strength
to pull herself free, even to share something nice.

"C'mon, it'll make you feel better," Archer said,
his tone firm but encouraging.

"Since when did you start moonlighting as a thera-
pist," Marissa said, irritation washing over her for his
refusal to let her just remain in the mood she was in.
"I don't want to talk right now."

"That's exactly why you should," he countered.

"I think I prefer the gruff, insensitive jackass to the Dr. Phil version of Archer Brant," she muttered. "That Archer Brant would've just let me be depressed."

"I'm going to let that slide, because I know you're hurting. C'mon. Trust me. Besides, I'm curious. You have to remember I only knew the wild side of your sister, the one who was always kicking up trouble and driving you crazy. Tell me something I don't know about the woman."

"She wasn't always kicking up trouble," Marissa said, frowning, even though she knew Mercedes had been a handful. There was something rude about talking ill of the dead. Mama would turn over in her grave if she knew.

"So disabuse me of that impression," he challenged.

He was transparent. She knew what he was doing but the drive was long, and if she remained in this morose mood she might do something completely idiotic like run screaming back to the Bay Area just to try and reclaim what had been taken from her, so she huffed an annoyed breath and picked a favorite memory to share.

She started off by grumbling, "You're a pain," and then sighed as she began. "Well, since Mercedes and I were only thirteen months apart—fertility seems to run in the family—we often wore the same clothes and shoes, which was a good thing seeing as Mama couldn't afford to buy much in spite of working two jobs. When I was fifteen I was asked to the senior prom by this senior, Hector Gonzalez. Of course, Mercedes was also asked to the prom but there was no way Mama could afford two dresses. I begged Mama but she said no. I was too young, and since Mercedes was older, she should get the dress. I was heartbroken but what could I say? So when we went to go shopping for Mercedes's dress I tried to stay home but Mercedes insisted that I go. I hated her for making me. And then she made me try on dresses with her, saying it would make it more fun. I pouted, whined and made a general pain of myself until finally, I gave up and just tried to have fun. And it was fun trying on the dresses. Mercedes picked my favorite dress and we left."

"That's your favorite memory?" Archer looked at her quizzically but she silenced him with a glare. "Sorry. Keep going."

"So we get home and Mercedes levels with me. The dress was for me. She told Mama she would stay home so I could go to my first prom. Mercedes said it was a big deal for a senior to ask a sophomore and she didn't want me to miss out. Besides, she could always go next year."

"Was it worth it? The prom?"

"It was amazing. Hector was a perfect gentleman and I felt like a princess." She smiled at the memory. Archer was right, she was starting to feel better. She gave him a smile, which he returned. Her insides melted just a little.

"So did Mercedes end up going to the prom the following year?" Archer asked.

"Ah, no, actually. She dropped out of high school her senior year," Marissa said, biting her lip. "That was the year Mama got sick. Mercedes dropped out to take care of Mama and me."

"Wasn't your sister only seventeen at the time?"

"Yes. At first she went on independent study, but then, she just stopped trying to make an effort to graduate. And the school didn't have time to waste on another Latina from the East Side. They probably figured she'd just gotten pregnant and that's why she dropped out. They didn't care." Marissa couldn't keep the bitterness from her voice but she tried to let it go, just the same. Mercedes was no longer in a place where those things mattered. No one could judge her any longer. "That's why it was so important for me to graduate, go to college. So I could help shoulder the load. To pay it back. You know?"

"Yeah. I do."

Marissa sighed. "It wasn't supposed to be like this. I had everything planned. Me and Mercedes were going to get a small condo—I'd already put aside a good down payment—all I needed to do was to get Mercedes away from Ruben. But he was like a disease, infecting her with his charm and evil ways. He turned her into someone else."

"Were drugs involved?"

Marissa didn't answer. She didn't have to. Archer heard the truth in her silence. He shook his head. "It happens, Rissa. Even the best of them fall sometimes," he said, trying to ease the burden she carried.

"Ruben got her into that lifestyle," Marissa said. Just saying his name made her want to vomit. "The swanky parties at the compound, Cristal champagne flowing like water, diamonds and other jewels given as payment for services rendered…it was Sodom and Gomorrah up there and Mercedes was sucked in. Every night after work I'd light a candle for her at St. Thomas Aquinas and pray for Mercedes to find a way out of that life before it killed her. I thought my prayers had been answered when she finally decided to leave Ruben but—" Her throat constricted and she had to look away. "I guess I was wrong," she managed to say before the tears made it impossible.

Archer swore softly and she glanced at him, confused. "What?" she asked.

"I've gone and upset you again. I was trying to make you feel better. Now you're crying. I'm sorry," he said. "I didn't realize how bad things were… toward the end."

"It's okay." Marissa wiped at her eyes. "I'm fine."

"You're not fine. Let's talk about something else," he suggested.

Marissa didn't want to talk any longer. It wasn't Archer's fault but her heart was too heavy to attempt more light conversation. She shook her head but her gaze softened when she met his worried stare. "If you don't mind, I'm just going to close my eyes for a little while. I didn't sleep well last night and...I'm exhausted," she said.

"Yeah, go ahead," Archer said but the worry was still in his eyes. And she loved him for it. Was that bad? She was too emotionally wrung out to try and figure it out.

CHAPTER TWELVE

THE SUN WAS RAPIDLY sinking into the bruised western sky when they arrived at Josh's cabin. The air held a bite to it that immediately had her bundling Jenna against the chill while Archer went in search of the hidden key.

She'd never been to Yosemite, much less the neighboring Wawona, so it was hard not to be taken in by the breathtaking sequoia trees, the ambient noise of the forest as it surrounded them and the chunks of granite that littered the area as if a giant had played marbles with them and then just left them behind when he was finished. The air nipped at her lungs but it was exhilarating.

Jenna voiced her displeasure with the chilly conditions and made her feelings known with a whimper as she tried burrowing deeper within the blanket tucked around her. "It's cold but so beautiful, *mija,*" she murmured against the baby's forehead.

Archer opened the front door and gestured. "Let's get you guys inside before you turn into Popsicles," he said and ushered them into the cabin.

It was an odd home. That was the first thing Marissa thought as she entered the long breezeway that by the looks of it was probably an add-on to the original building. A bedroom splintered off to the left and the living quarters were to the right. She waited as Archer secured the door and then followed him as he went to the front, checking windows as he went.

"No screens on these old houses so I always double-check the latch. I think we're safe here but old habits die hard."

She was thankful for his diligence. He made her feel safe even if it was an illusion. "Where's the heat?" she asked, shivering. It felt as cold inside as it did outside.

"Over here," he said, going over to a circular '50s model wall thermometer. He moved the small plastic knob to seventy-five and then disappeared into what she assumed was a bedroom. He emerged with two quilts. Then after wrapping one around her and Jenna, he disappeared again. This time she decided to follow.

The hardwood, scuffed and worn from many generations of families and vacationers, creaked under their weight but the sound was comforting, not unlike the sound an old wicker rocking chair makes when you sit in it, and Marissa recognized the rustic charm of this place. She entered a bedroom and smiled at the quaint white eyelet bedspread with matching bedskirt and the antique rosewood wardrobe that she guessed if she opened would smell faintly of moth-balls.

"This place is wonderful," she said, watching as he wrestled something from the small closet. "What is that?"

"A traveling crib," he answered, wresting it free with a heave as the motion dislodged a small vacuum cleaner that looked as old as the hardwood. He returned the vacuum and then made quick work of the small crib. He was only slightly flushed when he finished. "The Halvorsens keep it here for the families with young children. I figured you might need it for Jenna," he said.

"Thank you," she said, appreciation for his thoughtfulness warming her heart more quickly than the handmade quilt tucked around them. "Where will you sleep?" she asked.

He pointed down the hall. "There's another bedroom right there," he said, and she tried to hide her disappointment. Was it terrible that she wanted him to sleep beside her? This time it wasn't about sex, just about having his arms around her, making her feel protected and far from harm. Should she offer to let him stay with her? Would that make him uncomfortable? Her tongue felt tied and twisted and she couldn't quite believe that she was acting as jittery as a teenager with her first crush. They were both adults; they'd once been a couple…it wasn't so far-fetched to—

"What's wrong?" he asked, cutting into her mental rambling. Her head jerked at his question and she bit the side of her cheek, still not quite sure if she ought to just thank him and close the door or invite him to stay with her. "Marissa?"

"Stay with me," she blurted and her cheeks burned. Well, that was one way to get it out there. Not very suave. Not very subtle. Oh, well. She supposed they were way past those niceties anyway.

Archer hesitated but she could see a war going on behind those piercing blue eyes and she didn't know which side was winning, only she hoped it was the side she was on. "Arch?" She swallowed, feeling the silence fill the room. Oh, mercy. She'd made a terrible mistake. "You don't have to," she said quickly. "I just—"

"If it's what you want, I will stay here with you," he said, coming to stand within kissing distance. She could feel his breath on her cheek and her eyelids threatened to flutter closed but she forced them to remain open and wide. He caressed the side of her cheek with a gentle touch as he said, "Marissa, I would like nothing more than to spend the night curled beside you but you can't play with my heart."

"I'm not," she stammered, not quite sure where he was going with this. "I wouldn't…"

He held her gaze. "What happens when this is all over? When you don't need me anymore? Am I going to be a complication you don't want like before?"

Stung, she drew away. "I didn't do that."

"You did," he disagreed. "But I'm willing to let that be in the past if you can tell me that's not how it will be in the future."

She swallowed, her mouth worked but the words had dried up. What could she tell him? What promises could she make? "What are you asking me?" she asked, stalling for time to think of how to answer a question she didn't truly have the answer for. She didn't know what the future entailed. There were too many variables to even try and formulate an educated guess.

"Marissa, I'm asking if I'm going to be a part of your life for the long haul or am I just your temporary bodyguard with privileges?"

"I don't know. Please don't make me answer that right now," she pleaded. "You have no idea how things are going to turn out with all this. I know you're hoping for the best but there's a worst-case scenario, too, and I can't ignore the possibility that we might not be so lucky with the outcome. So, I'm not about to make a promise I don't know if I can keep."

Dissatisfaction with her answer darkened his expression and his mouth tightened but he seemed to understand her reasoning. He stepped away and Marissa's heart contracted painfully as if they were tethered together and the movement strained the cord. "Fine. But as you're factoring all the variables into your calculations, try to remember this—I'm not the one who walked away from this relationship. Not then. Not now."

"That's not fair," she whispered. Jenna, sensing the tension, shifted in her arms and whimpered. Archer's gaze rested on the baby for a moment and for an instant Marissa could see this man loving a child who wasn't his. For all his tough act, he was soft and sweet on the inside. Just for catching that glimpse she might've been tempted to give him the answer he needed but he deserved her honesty even if it hurt them both to hear it. "You've said your piece. Thank you. Perhaps it's better that you sleep in the other bedroom," she said stiffly, though her heart wailed and protested, nearly causing her to rescind the words and offer different ones.

His lips all but disappeared as he compressed them, keeping whatever it was he wanted to say behind his teeth. She had a feeling that was a blessing.

"Fine. There's likely no food in the fridge or pantry. We'll have to make do with what we brought in the ice chest until we get down to the market tomorrow morning. Is there anything else you need?" he asked with all the solicitous courtesy of a man paid to do a job, nothing more, nothing less.

She tried not to show that his withdrawal hurt but she was a terrible actress and it was likely written all over her face. "We're good. Thank you, Archer," she offered, hoping the words softened the tension between them.

It didn't.

IT WAS LATE. Archer tossed on the hard mattress, stifling a groan at being unable to find a spot that didn't make his back or shoulder scream. He wasn't cut out for this kind of roughing it any longer. He rolled to his back and stared at the darkened ceiling. He thought he understood Marissa's reluctance to commit due to the circumstances but she didn't say that if things were different she'd jump into his arms. He sensed her hanging back, keeping a part of herself separate, just as she did when they were engaged and that didn't make him feel very secure in her feelings. Sex was one thing but to run the risk of sounding like a chick, there was more to life than a good roll in the sack.

And he wanted whatever that might entail. He'd thought he'd wanted it back then, but he'd been just as stubborn about the whole job thing as she was being about the circumstances between them. He'd assumed she'd follow him, like a good wife. Hell, he'd been wrong. And frankly, it had been arrogant of him to assume any such thing. Now, he'd never ask her to give up her career, yet, in essence, he'd have to give up his line of work in order to make things happen with Marissa.

He waited for the sharp pang to hit at the thought

of leaving behind the special ops division. The only
pang he felt was the dull ache from his shoulder.
What did that mean? Was he ready to move on? Get
a nine to five? Okay, there was the shudder he'd been
waiting for. So, not your typical day job but maybe
something that didn't involve someone shooting at
him on a regular basis.

And what was that? He didn't know. But he supposed he could find out. To what end? Marissa wasn't
even meeting him halfway. Why should he rearrange
his life completely when she wasn't even willing to
take a few steps in his direction?

He grabbed the second pillow and punched it a few
times to fluff it up but it was an old feather pillow and
all it did was burp out a few tufts of fluff. He sneezed
and then tucked the pillow under the first pillow in
the hopes of creating more comfort. Useless. Sleep
wasn't going to happen for him tonight.

And it was a long way until morning.

He groaned softly and tried a little meditation.
One, two, three… Who says this stuff worked? God
help him.

It was going to be a long night.

MARISSA AWOKE, EVERY muscle stiff and a headache
pounding from behind her left eyeball. So much for
the healthy benefits of sleeping in Mother Nature's
bosom. She rose on her elbows and glanced down at
the sleeping form of the toddler in the crib. She

smiled. At least Jenna didn't seem to mind the accommodations. As she went to return to the bed, perhaps to grab a few more minutes of sleep, a mouthwatering, tantalizing smell jerked her back up and out of the bed. Slipping into her jeans and sweatshirt, she padded into the tiny kitchen to find Archer hard at work at the old porcelain stove, whisking a creamy white gravy that smelled like heaven and made the saliva fill her mouth. "If you have fresh biscuits in that oven I will kiss you," she said before catching herself. She almost groaned out loud. "I'm sorry…"

He waved away her apology. "Get ready to eat," he directed and she didn't waste time. In the dining room, where an antique table commanded the space, she grabbed the cutlery and laid out a makeshift place setting.

Archer came in with two plates, one laden with bacon, the other eggs. Then returned with the biscuits and gravy.

She eyed the spread with suspicion. "I thought you said there was no food in the house." She gestured to the plates. "I'd say this is a pretty good sampling of breakfast goodies."

"While you were still sleeping I went down to the Pine Tree Market for some food to last us a few days if need be. A good breakfast is important to start the day off right. Dish up."

Marissa didn't wait but she grumbled at his good mood. "You must've slept better than me," she said, stuffing a thick-cut piece of bacon in her mouth. "You're too perky for someone who only caught a few winks." *Like me.*

His mouth twitched as if holding back a smile but he didn't comment. Instead, he said, "I was thinking we should take a walk down to the river. It's beautiful this time of year."

"The river?" she asked, frowning at the idea of taking a toddler down by a river. She hated to admit it but she was a city girl. She'd never been around rivers or lakes growing up. There was a city pool but she could never afford the admission fee and she hadn't had a bathing suit worth letting others see, but the biggest reason and the reason that made little shivers of dread dance down her spine was the very plain fact that she couldn't swim. "I think I'll pass," she murmured before stuffing a bite of gravy-soaked biscuit in her mouth.

But Archer wasn't about to let it go. "C'mon, there's a swinging bridge and it's really quaint. It might take your mind off things. I think we could all use a change of scenery."

"This is a change of scenery."

"I mean, it would be nice to be outside. Enjoy the sunshine. We've been cooped up in the house for days and I feel like I'm starting to mold."

"I said no," she snapped. Then horrified at her own waspishness, pulled herself back to offer a quiet, "No, thank you."

Archer stared at her, trying to gauge where that came from, and just when she was sure he was going to call her on it, he returned to his breakfast with a shrug. "It was just an idea."

They ate in silence for a few more minutes until the guilt made it impossible to ignore. Putting down her fork, she stared at her plate and when she thought she could bear to admit how embarrassed she was with her own lack of skill, she said in a tight voice, "I don't know how to swim."

He looked up startled. "Excuse me?"

She gave him a pained look. "You're going to make me say it again? Can't you see how hard it was for me to admit that?"

He held up his hand and calmed her quickly building annoyance at what appeared to be thick-headedness, and said, "I heard you…I'm just not quite sure where the admission came from. It's too cold to swim, Rissa. I certainly wouldn't suggest that you jump in the water. That's snow water and bound to freeze your butt off."

"I know you weren't suggesting we go for a dip," Marissa said, frustrated. "I just mean that I don't feel comfortable being so close to a raging water source when I don't even know how to doggy-paddle. What if I slipped? What if by some horrible circumstance, Jenna fell in? How would I save her if I couldn't save myself?"

"I would save you or the baby if either of those

situations occurred," he answered simply and if she hadn't been so pissed off and overtired, she would've laughed at his earnest declaration. He shrugged. "What's the big deal? I'm trained in water rescue, you know."

"That's not the point," she maintained, pushing away her plate, wishing she had room in her belly for more food, since it had been so delicious. "The point is...well, I can't always expect you to be there to save me so I should avoid putting myself into situations where I can't save myself."

"Fair enough," he agreed briskly, surprising her with his quick capitulation. Too quick, she thought. Then he leaned over and pressed a firm kiss to her lips, startling her with the action. He smiled at her bewildered expression, prompting him to explain. "You said if there were biscuits in the oven you'd kiss me. I was just collecting on what you'd already offered."

Sneaky fox, she thought, but it warmed her to her toes. She risked a small smile. "Imagine what I might've done if you'd somehow procured chocolate macadamia muffins."

She slid out of the chair with her dirty plate before he could snag another kiss and scooped up his, as well. "It's only fair that I pick up the kitchen duty since you cooked. There's only one catch, you need to go wake up Jenna and feed her while I wash and dry. Deal?"

He seemed uncertain but only for a second. "I can handle that. Dish soap and drying rack are under the counter."

Marissa smiled and went to clean up. As she filled the small sink and prepared to scrub their breakfast plates and pans, she was struck by how much she enjoyed this simple scene of domestic unity. She'd grown up without a father in her life, with only Mama and Mercedes to keep her company and shape her ideals. She wondered how not having a strong male figure in their lives steered their decisions as adults. Her thoughts strayed to Jenna, whom she could hear giggling and burbling to Archer who was doing his best to get her to eat eggs and bites of biscuit by alternately talking to her like an adult and then when that didn't work, tried talking to her in a high-pitched voice that made Marissa wonder if he'd lost a testicle somewhere. And then she wondered if Jenna would suffer without someone in her life to call Daddy.

Ruben was her father, a voice reminded her, and she winced. If only she could erase that small detail. It wasn't as if he'd been an active participant in Jenna's life aside from the occasional dismissive glance her way when Mercedes had desperately tried to regain his favor with the child. Perhaps if Jenna had been a boy, he'd said, his lip curling at the child he'd given life to without a second thought. Marissa burned inside at the idea of Jenna growing up at the compound, surrounded by thugs, rapists and drug pushers, all on Ruben's payroll.

Finished, she rounded the corner to find Archer rolling around on the living room floor with Jenna as she climbed all over him like a man-size jungle gym. It was hard not to smile at the fun they were having but Marissa was too keyed up to truly just enjoy the moment. "So, what's next?" she asked, rubbing her pruned fingers together, wishing for a split second she had her vanilla sugar-cookie lotion from back home. "Not that I don't enjoy playing house in the mountains, I can't take this uncertainty. We need to find out if Layla is okay. She wouldn't know how to handle someone like Ruben. He'll break her within seconds and have fun doing it."

Archer patted Jenna on her curly dark head and handed her the plastic hot dog—the one toy Marissa had managed to grab before they bolted from the house—to play with, and then rolled to his haunches, all playfulness gone. She shivered at his ability to turn off and on. "I called Rico this morning. The problem is that we're not involved in an official investigation. The channels normally available to us are closed. We're sneaking around, hacking into secured networks, looking for ways to bring this dirtbag down, but in the meantime Rico is also looking for your friend."

Marissa swallowed. "Looking? As in you can't find her?"

Archer looked grim and the bottom of Marissa's world dropped out. "She's not at home?" she asked, desperate thoughts fuzzing rationality and all sense of self-preservation. "We have to go to the city. I know where she hangs out, where her mother lives…I could maybe—"

"I can't let you do that," Archer said. "It's not safe."

"I don't care. Layla didn't ask for this. She's an innocent person who got sucked into this mess by a careless phone call I made. We have to help her."

"And we will but I'm not about to let you walk back into that viper's nest and get yourself killed…or worse."

"He won't hurt me." Much. He doesn't like his girls to have marks. She couldn't hold back the shudder. Once, with his hands tucked into leather gloves he'd punched Mercedes in the stomach when she was pregnant. It hadn't left a mark, nor had it caused her to abort—much to his disappointment.

"You don't know what he'll do," Archer countered, a glitter in his eyes that she knew wasn't meant for her. "And I'm not about to take that chance. Besides, you have to stop and think what that will mean for Jenna. She needs you more than Layla right now."

She couldn't argue that. Defeat made her slump in the chair nearest her but fear quickened her heart for Layla's safety.

"Rico is looking for her. I trust him. I need you to trust me."

"It's not that I don't—" She stopped, tears filling her eyes. She wiped them away, angry with herself for being so close to crying all the time. "I just want my life back and the harder I hope and pray, the more it seems things will never be the same. If Layla…"

"Don't play the what-if game," he warned, his voice suddenly hard. She sat a little straighter, watching him for clues as to what was going through his head. "You deal in facts. The facts are these— Layla is not where she should be. She could be with Ruben. She could be taking a personal day, spending it at the mall. There's no sense in playing what-if when we don't know all the facts. Period."

She jerked a short nod. There was logic in that. Layla had been talking about taking a personal day now that the first phase of her projects was finished. Marissa licked her lips and tried to take a deep calming breath. It could be pure coincidence that Layla was not where she should be when Marissa's life was imploding with Ruben at the center of it.

It sounded rational. Logical. Plausible.

Yet, there was a sick feeling lodged in her stomach that told her otherwise.

St. Jude have mercy!

ARCHER WAS TRYING TO follow his own advice but he had information that he'd withheld from Marissa so as not to further upset her. Layla's apartment had been trashed. According to Rico, there were definite signs of a struggle.

He was simply waiting for word. And he was starting to believe it was time to bring in the feds. Officially.

It was after lunch when the phone finally rang. Archer answered on the first ring, not wanting either Marissa or Jenna to wake from their naps. Archer had instructed Marissa to try and catch some winks with the baby, and given the dark bags under her eyes, he wasn't surprised when she didn't fight him on it.

"Bad news." Was all Rico said. He didn't need to elaborate.

"Dead?"

"Her body was found in a Dumpster on the East Side. She was pretty messed up, Arch."

Rico's quiet statement put lead weights in his gut. "Give me the details, what you know and how you know it."

"A homeless man found her body when he was digging for recyclables. She was bloody and bruised. I talked with the M.E. and he confirmed rape and sodomy. Cause of death looks like strangulation but that's not official, of course, just an educated guess by the M.E."

"Did you flash your badge to get this info?"

"Didn't have to. The M.E. and I go way back. She volunteered the information as a courtesy to our history together. But I think it's time to bring in the team," Rico advised, echoing the very thing Archer had been thinking earlier. "I know you're worried about the complications with the kid, but this guy's a rabid dog and he needs to be put down. You savvy?"

"Yeah," Archer sighed. They were out of time and options. Marissa wasn't going to like this but if there was any hope of catching this guy, they were going to need more artillery than Archer had on his own. "Go ahead and let the General know what's going down. I'll await the orders."

Archer hung up and wondered how he was going to break the news to Marissa about her friend. He supposed the best way was to just get it over with, like ripping a bandage in one jerk instead of trying to pull it inch by excruciating inch. Except, he didn't know how much more Marissa could stand. She seemed fragile, near to her breaking point and he couldn't stand being the one to give her the news that would make her shatter.

CHAPTER THIRTEEN

MARISSA AWOKE FROM her nap more refreshed and feeling more in control of herself than earlier and she focused on staying optimistic. Archer was right; she couldn't assume she knew what happened to Layla just because bad things were happening to her personally. It didn't mean Layla was caught in the same web of misfortune.

Rising, she checked on Jenna who was still sleeping soundly, then went in search of Archer.

She found him cleaning his gun at the antique table. The sight of that cold, dark metal made her insides shake and all that fledgling optimism fled in the face of her reality.

"Rissa, I have bad news," he said, and the strength seeped from her legs so that she sat abruptly in the chair next to him. He paused to finish and then when it was cleaned to his satisfaction, he holstered the piece and then met her terrified gaze. "It's about Layla."

"No," she moaned, her heart squeezing so hard it hurt to breathe. "Don't tell me."

"I have to tell you."

"She's dead, isn't she?" she asked, her voice curiously calm in spite of the feeling that she might pass out.

"Yes. Her body was found in a Dumpster on the East Side this morning. Her family has confirmed the identification."

"Was she…" She could barely get the words out but she needed to know. "Was she…"

Archer knew what she was trying to say. He nodded gravely. "Yes."

Marissa buried her face in her hands as she drew deep, sucking breaths but couldn't seem to get enough air. "She…she…didn't deserve… this…Archer. It's m-my fault," she said, her teeth starting to chatter from a raw mixture of anger, grief and fear. "I should've warned her that I was in trouble…that she shouldn't talk to anyone who came looking for me. I should've…but I didn't because I wanted to be able to return to my life. It was so selfish of me. Archer…I put her in harm's way just like Mercedes put me and Jenna. I'm no different than my sister."

"I'm sorry about your friend," Archer offered softly and she tried to draw comfort from his understanding. "But this isn't your fault. You did what you thought was best for everyone. You had no way of knowing it would come to this. Don't take that on."

If not her, then who? She shook her head. "You

don't understand. Layla...she was so sweet and nice. She always had a smile for everyone. We used to joke that she was probably incapable of mustering the appropriate facial expression to fire someone. She was so happy. She wouldn't have recognized Ruben as anything but a nice guy because she always saw the good in someone." She balled her fists, wanting desperately to beat something but she kept them in her lap. She let out a long, halting breath then looked to Archer, who still seemed as if there was more bad news to come. "What?" she asked. "What else is there?"

He didn't answer right away. That in itself made her go very still, waiting for the next shoe to drop. When he did start talking again, she wished she could just cover her ears and wish it all away. "Things have gotten out of control, Rissa. This guy is a cancer and he's got to be taken out."

"Yeah, you and what army are going to accomplish this?" Marissa snorted, still angry. "He's untouchable."

"No one is untouchable," Archer disagreed.

"You don't know Ruben."

"I don't have to. I've known plenty of Ruben-type characters and I've sent plenty to rot in prison."

"And how many got away?" she challenged, not impressed with his previous statement. She didn't need machismo, not right now. Archer's hard look might've sent someone else scurrying for cover but

Marissa was too keyed up to care. "What about that injury on your shoulder? Did you put away the guy who gave you that? Or did he get away?" Archer's nostrils flared but he remained silent. It didn't matter. She read him easily. "You can't catch them all, Archer," she said. "That's just life."

"I can sure as hell try," he said stiffly. "And I will catch the person who gave me this little souvenir. You can count on it."

She looked away. "Yeah, well, Ruben isn't a one-man assignment. It would take a legion to take him down."

"You're right," he said, surprising her with his easy agreement. He didn't make her wait long for the reason. "That's why I've brought in the feds."

"You did what?" She jumped from the chair, the adrenaline surging through her body to give her the strength she'd lost only moments ago. "Why'd you do that? What did you tell them about Jenna and..." She struggled to even say his name her fear was so great. "And M-Manny?"

"I told them everything."

She searched his face to see if he was lying. When she saw that he wasn't she wanted to scream, pummel his face and run. He must've read all of that in her expression for he was quick on his feet, coming toward her to grip both shoulders in a gentle but firm hold. "Marissa," he said, looking into her eyes, "this is serious. He's involved with the killing of two people but we have to have proof and the only way to get it is to open an investigation."

"The FBI isn't going to take this seriously. They're just going to turn it over to the local authorities and Ruben has them in his pocket," she said bitterly, shrugging out of his grasp. "You might as well just let me walk right back into that compound and hand over Jenna and myself. That's going to be the end result anyway and I'd rather do it on my terms."

"No, that's not going to happen," Archer said, his voice sharp but she didn't care. "We're going to catch that son of a bitch and put him away for a long time."

"Promise?" she taunted him. "No? Can't make promises, can you? So don't. I'm going home. And you can't stop me."

"Don't do this, Marissa," he fairly pleaded, and that shocked her. Archer didn't beg or plead. She looked away from the conflict shining in his eyes, not wanting to see the worry there. "I can help you but you have to let me do it my way," he said.

"We tried that and my friend was killed. Your way sucks."

She turned and started to walk away but Archer grabbed her arm and pulled her to him. She barely had time to gasp before Archer's mouth was on hers. Her body went on autopilot, sliding and melting, as her tongue clashed with his, her passion fueled by rage and terror. Her brain ceased to think of anything other than the sensation of being pressed up against

Archer's hard chest and she gave in to the pleasure—
until she felt the cold bite of steel clicking around her
wrists. She jerked away and stared at the handcuff encircling her small wrist. "What are you doing?" she
cried out, not quite able to believe what she was
seeing. But it was very real and he had already
clamped her other wrist by the time she thought to
struggle. "Archer? What's going on?"

Archer's expression had gone flat as he answered,
his tone all business. "I can't let you leave. I have in-
structions that if you don't come willingly, I must
take you into federal custody on the charges of kidnapping at the very least. I won't lie…second degree
murder might be applicable if Manny did, in fact, die.
Take a seat while I load the car."

"You bastard," she hissed, spitting mad on the
surface but gravely wounded on the inside by his
betrayal. She wished a thousand deaths on his head
for his two-faced lies of protection. A horrible
thought came at her sidewise. What if he'd planned
this all along? What if his hatred for her went so
deep that he'd been willing to manufacture concern
for her just so he could make the final blow that
much more painful? In her jumbled, heartbroken
haze, it was completely plausible and the more she
gave it air, the more the idea took root. She'd slept
with him, gave him her heart, fantasized about living
a life with him. All of that plus the fact that he'd
wormed his way somehow into Jenna's little heart

made her want to plunge a knife straight into the cavity where his own heart should've been if he'd had one. Oh, it hurt. Hurt like nothing she'd ever known and she wanted to make him pay somehow but she was helpless at the moment and likely heading to prison, so her dreams of revenge were useless. Unable to do anything more, she simply screamed, "You lying, sneaky bastard! I can't believe the depths of your cruelty. I hate you!"

Archer's expression didn't change, even in the face of her condemnation, nor did he offer anything in his defense. No, the coward just walked away, leaving her to fume and quake in fear—all alone.

ARCHER FELT SICK BUT he stuffed it down so he could focus. He was doing this for her own good, her protection. He wished he could let her in on the plan that he and Rico had come up with but there was no guarantee the General was going to let them follow through so he'd kept it to himself. Besides, it was a risky plan, one that put Marissa directly in harm's way but it might be the only way to save her.

In the end, she might still hate him but she'd be alive. And that's all that mattered.

The ride was deadly silent. Even Jenna seemed to realize something bad was going on for she remained quiet throughout the drive. Eventually, she dropped off to sleep and Archer was relieved. He hated having her around so much tension. In a very short time, he'd

gotten close to the kid. He wasn't about to let anything happen to her. He wasn't sure how to process
those feelings so he stuffed those down, too.

They drove straight to the headquarters in San
Francisco, to the nondescript gray building that on
the outside looked more like a condemned space
than something that housed a division of the FBI that
was highly irregular in their activities. He pulled
into an underground parking garage and shut off the
car.

"Is this where you drop me off and I get finger-
printed and sized for an orange jumpsuit?" she asked
coldly, refusing to look at him. Her handcuffed wrists
were held in front of her so she could ride comfort-
ably in the car.

He considered telling her what was happening but
he wanted to wait until he got the all clear from his
team. He ignored her jab and got out of the car. Rico
appeared at the elevator and came toward them.

Archer unlatched Marissa's seat belt and helped
her out of the car. Next, he went to the backseat and
gently freed a sleeping Jenna from her car seat. Then,
in a move he knew would put Marissa over the edge,
he handed the baby to Rico.

"What's going on?" Marissa demanded. She
speared Archer with a look that promised retribution
if a hair on Jenna's head was damaged, but there
were tears in her eyes that he wanted to wipe away.
She started to move toward Rico and Archer stepped

in her way. "Get out of my way, Archer," she said in a low tone.

"Rico, take the baby. I'll take Marissa," he said, his stare never leaving hers, not trusting her to stay put as she was told. He didn't need to watch to know that Rico was already melting into the shadows with the precious bundle.

"You tell me where he's taking her or so help me, Archer, I will kill you," she said, her voice tight. "I mean it."

"Settle down," he said gruffly, taking her by the arm as he walked her to the elevator. "She's going to be fine. You on the other hand might not be if you keep threatening a federal agent. There are laws against that, you know."

"Screw you," she said, full of piss and vinegar, rage and despair. "What's going to happen? Are you taking her back to Ruben?" She twisted in his grip to stare at him, her gaze pleading and filled with true fear, not for herself but for the baby. "He doesn't love her, doesn't even care about her. Please don't give her back to him. If she died, he wouldn't even blink. He'd be relieved! He never wanted her... Archer, please...don't give her back to that monster," she said, her voice tumbling to a pained whisper that even he couldn't ignore any longer. He pulled her into his arms and tucked her against his chest where she sagged in spite of her anger, shaking like a leaf in a stiff wind.

"Let's get you inside. We have to talk," he said, pressing a quick, almost illicit kiss against her crown. Her sharp intake of breath told him he'd shocked her with the action, probably even confused her. He could do nothing else. The success of this plan required Marissa to be unaware—at least at the beginning—of the plan.

CHAPTER FOURTEEN

MARISSA WAS LED TO a small, square room with gray walls that matched the gray, metal table, and gray floor tile. It was probably the most uncomfortable room she'd ever had the misfortune to be put into but something told her that was the point. She'd never had so much as a traffic ticket yet here she was handcuffed in federal custody.

She tried not to shiver but her skin danced with goose pimples from the chill conditions and her nerves. She swallowed hard when a suit-dressed man, tall and lean with a polished air, walked into the room.

"Hello, Marissa," he said evenly, taking a seat and gesturing for her to do the same. When she'd reluctantly slid into the metal chair, he continued in a voice that was firm, authoritative, yet oddly soothing. "I'm Agent Hawker but you can call me Jeremiah. Do you know why you're here?"

Kidnapping was the easy answer but she'd seen enough crime dramas to know that she didn't need to admit to anything without a lawyer present. Still,

Jeremiah Hawker had a way of making her feel like he was on her side…even if she knew that was impossible. "No," she finally answered.

His slow, easy smile said *I know you're lying*. "Let me help you out," he began, unperturbed by her lack of cooperation. "Seems you took something that didn't quite belong to you and possibly killed a man even though I suspect the circumstances were a bit on the extreme side. You lost your sister recently?"

Marissa nodded, biting her lip to keep it from quivering. Jeremiah nodded in turn, sympathy in his stare.

"I'm sorry for your loss." And the way he said it almost made her believe he meant it until he continued, "But even if we put aside the situation with Ruben's cousin until we receive further information, you still took a child and that's a crime. You understand that, right?"

She compressed her lips together, hating Archer for bringing them here to face this smooth-talking executioner. "I want a lawyer," she said.

He smiled. "We're just talking."

"And we're done talking until I get a lawyer."

He spread his hands as if in surrender but she wasn't that naive to think that he was giving in that easily. "Sure. We'll get you a lawyer. I just wanted to give you an opportunity to make a deal but if you want to bring in the dogs, we'll toss out the meat and see what happens next."

"What does that mean?" she asked, her brow furrowing. That didn't sound like it ended well for the meat. "I have rights… I want to talk to Archer."

He sat straighter, his expression going from bland and soft to hard and unyielding. "Marissa Vasquez, you've broken the law. Even criminal scumbags like Ruben Ortiz have the right to their children until a court of law determines otherwise. It's within our rights to prosecute you for kidnapping…" There was a *but* hanging on to the end of his declaration and she felt herself holding her breath. He stood, then shrugged. "But it seems Mr. Ortiz doesn't want to press charges."

The blood in her face drained and she felt woozy. "What?"

"Seems Mr. Ortiz has a bigger heart than you realized. Maybe he's turned over a new leaf. Anyway, it doesn't matter. According to Mr. Ortiz, his cousin is fine and has since gone home to Puerto Rico. You're free to go as soon as Mr. Ortiz is finished signing paperwork. You're a lucky woman."

"He's here?" she nearly gasped, fear pounding her heart like a drum.

He waved away her question as he unlocked the handcuffs. "Downstairs in the public area," he said. Tossing the cuffs on the table, the loud clatter made her jump and he winked. She drew back, unsure of what the hell kind of signals this man was sending her but fairly certain she wanted away from this place. He gestured for her to follow and she did, taking the elevator down.

They exited the elevator and entered a quiet reception area. The hair on Marissa's arms stood at attention as Ruben's voice carried as he entered with Archer.

They were laughing as if they were the best of friends—and it made her blood boil. Her gaze flicked to Archer, seething and uncomprehending of the scene in front of her—and then moved to Ruben, nearly flinching when he swiveled to catch her stare.

His grin broadened and he opened his arms in welcome. She fought to keep from running in the opposite direction. She lifted her chin—fear was like a drug to Ruben and she wasn't going to give him the satisfaction—and faced him, acknowledging him coolly.

"Marissa…why have you done this foolish thing?" he asked, his tone gently chiding but the heat in his eyes burned with a promise of retribution. "We are like family, you and I. I was distraught with worry, *cariño.*"

Marissa looked to Archer to gauge his reaction but he remained impassive, as if watching the reunion of complete strangers. Ruben continued as if she hadn't silently rebuffed his attempt at reconciliation, saying, "Well, not to worry. You and the baby will come home. Where is my daughter, Agent Brant?"

It was then Archer affected an apologetic expression as he said, "I'm sorry, we can't release the child until she's had a full physical by the pediatrician. Standard protocol. She'll be in federal custody for a day or two and then we can release her to you, provided she's given the all clear."

Ruben pondered this for a moment but it was all for effect. Marissa knew that Jenna was a minor inconvenience to him. She was the real prize. So she wasn't surprised when he smiled and nodded as if he understood the protocol and was willing to abide by it. Of course, he was willing. It got Jenna out of his hair for the time being until he decided what to do with her. Marissa didn't think for a minute that Ruben was suddenly pining to be a father.

"I have my own home, Ruben," she said clearly and there it was, the flash of rage she'd known was hiding under that slick exterior. But he banked it quickly in the presence of the federal agents. Since he was putting on an act, she thought she'd join in with her own Oscar-worthy performance. She offered a grateful smile. "I appreciate your offer. I'm sorry I worried you. I wasn't thinking straight with the death of my sister so fresh. All I could think of was finding her *dead body* and it messed with my mind," she said, putting a very subtle emphasis on *dead body* knowing he'd catch it even if no one else did. His stare narrowed but he countered with an indulgent smile.

"All is forgiven. Just come home with me. Let me

take care of you. It's all I want to do," he said. "It's the least I can do. You know I cared deeply for your sister."

Bullshit. She caught herself seconds before the world flew from her mouth.

"It's settled. I have a car outside," he said.

Ruben, believing the matter finished, thanked the agents for the timely and safe return of the daughter he couldn't give two figs for and, sliding his designer sunglasses onto his face, walked out the door.

Archer moved to her, ignoring her look of open hostility and said, "If you'll just come with me a moment, we'll get you signed out."

She wanted to scream at him but she was tongue-tied by overwhelming sorrow that seemed to spill over her anger, as crazy as that sounded. Perhaps it was the fact that Ruben was likely to kill her—when he'd tired of her—and she didn't want her last conversation with Archer to be one filled with hatred.

He gripped her elbow and steered her solicitously to a desk with paperwork strewn about and as he bent down to show her ostensibly where to sign, he whispered, "I need you to listen. I only have a minute. Ruben can't suspect a thing." He pressed something small and hard into her hand. "Put these on. They're wired."

He pulled away and she turned, giving him her back as she pretended to sign the paperwork and then glanced at what he'd put in her hand. They were tiny gold stud earrings. She trembled at the implication and her knees threatened to give out. Perhaps Archer hadn't sold her out. He was trying to catch Ruben the only way possible. Suddenly she understood. Her brain worked quickly. "Jenna is safe?" she murmured.

"As safe and secure as Fort Knox. He isn't going to get anywhere near her."

Relief made her weepy but her troubles were far from over. In fact, she still might not make it out alive but at least Jenna would be safe and that was something she knew Archer would make sure of.

She swallowed and caught the looks of Jeremiah and Archer, both intense in their regard, focused to the point of a sword. She whispered a prayer, and then she walked out the door to climb into Ruben's awaiting Town Car.

ARCHER BLEW OUT A measured breath, fighting to remain calm and relaxed until the Town Car pulled away.

His gut roiled at the act he'd played with Ortiz, laughing at his lame jokes and pretending to believe Ortiz was sophisticated and charming when all he wanted to do was put his fist through the man's face. Marissa's silent terror and Jenna's sweet face held him in check, forced him to focus on the big picture.

He whirled on Jeremiah. "Control room," he said,

sprinting to a room on the left where the surveillance tools were kept.

There was some static as they opened the channel and then the sound of Marissa's and Ruben's voices came through loud and clear.

"Who knew you were such a good actor," she said, her voice cutting.

"I have many talents, *cariño,*" was all Ruben said in return. "And I'm very much anticipating showing you just how talented I am with many things. Did you know I can cook? No? I make homemade tortillas just like Mama. Fresh and warm from the oven… they're to die for. Ah, but that's nothing. Cooking a meal is simple. Throw in the right ingredients and you're already halfway to success. No, my true talents are much harder to define, *cariño.*"

"Stop calling me that. I am not your darling."

"I will call you what I please," Ruben countered and it wasn't hard to hear the thread of malice weaving its way through his silky voice even over the wire. "And it pleases me to call you this. You are mine, Marissa."

Archer clenched his fists to keep from snarling, trying to stay in control of himself.

"Steady, Arch," Jeremiah warned, sensing the tension building. "We'll get him. He has no idea she's wired. He'll slip and then we'll get him."

Archer grunted an agreement, not trusting that he wouldn't snap at his friend.

Marissa's voice came on again. "I don't belong to anyone, much less you, Ruben."

Ruben chuckled. "That's where you're wrong. Because I have something you want more than anything in the world. Something you're willing to kill for. I admire that in a woman. Your fire and passion mirrors my own. We are meant to be together and now that your sister is no longer between us—"

A loud crack of a palm slapping flesh resounded through the wire and Archer knew Marissa had slapped Ruben. A wash of pride went through him. *That's my girl,* he thought, wishing he could've seen the man's face. That is until Ruben said, "You will pay for that, and so much more, *cariño.* This will be fun. So much more fun than what I did to your friend Layla. That was child's play compared to what I have in store for you."

"Sick bastard," Marissa said, her voice tight with pain. "Let go of me."

She gasped and Archer jumped to his feet, ready to get in the car and go after them right now, but Jeremiah caught him and gestured for him to stop. "He's not really hurting her and we don't have anything that will keep him behind bars for any longer than it takes his lawyer to rip through the processing paperwork. This is serious. Keep it cool, Brant."

Keep it cool? He glared at Jeremiah. If it were someone he cared about in that car he wouldn't be so calm and collected. He'd be wanting to rip the guy's head off, same as Archer felt right now. Damn it! But Jeremiah was right. They had to play it straight, otherwise, Marissa would never be free of that man's shadow and Jenna would likely go back to him.

"All right…but I swear to God, Jeremiah, if he so much as harms a hair on her head, I will personally put a bullet into his brain and I won't lose sleep over it."

In spite of Archer's vehement declaration, Jeremiah smirked, saying, "Yeah, imagine the paperwork on that screwup. It'll make the situation with Kandy Kane look like first-grade homework. Listen, I hear you, but I can't have you going all John Wayne on me. That's how people die. You don't want that. I know you don't. So don't make it happen. Be cool. Be straight. And everyone will walk away happy."

Archer looked away as he shoved both hands through his hair before he could acknowledge the solid advice his friend was giving him. But, hey, he wasn't a Mr. Nice and go-by-the-book kind of guy, so he said with a shrug, "You know I'm still going to kill him."

Jeremiah laughed. "Yeah. The General made me promise to give you the spiel so he didn't have to. If it comes down to that, I'm a hundred percent behind you, man. The world isn't going to miss one less Ruben Ortiz. He's one sick piece of shit."

If Jeremiah knew just how bad Ortiz was…he

might've shot the guy himself. The guy had an itchy trigger finger when it came to bad guys. It was one of his more endearing qualities.

CHAPTER FIFTEEN

MARISSA RUBBED HER wrist where Ruben had gripped her, twisting until she felt the bones cracking together, and shot him a dark look, full of the hatred she had for him.

"Ah, that fire." He chuckled. The sound of throaty appreciation tinged with lust made her shudder. "But now we must talk business. There have been some unfortunate situations since you left and at first I was very angry. Oh, so angry. I wanted to do very bad things, *cariño*. But now that you are home again… I'm feeling generous."

"I'm not going home with you. I have my own place."

He waved her statement away. "Your home is with me."

"You can't make me give up my apartment," she maintained stubbornly, trying to contain the tremor that was starting at her knees.

Ruben startled her when he leaned in very close. She instinctively drew back but the seat prevented her from going far. His eyes gleamed with delighted cruelty and she wondered if the man had lost his mind. His hand snaked up to grip her chin hard. She bit her lip to keep from crying out. "I can make you do anything I choose. I could whore you out like I did your sister, peddling that sweet flesh to the dirtiest men who ever crawled out of the East Side for a six-pack of Budweiser or I could make you dance at the club, showing your pretty tits and ass for a dollar."

She struggled against his grip and this time she couldn't keep the shake from her voice as she said, "You'll have to kill me. I'll never be your whore. Not for anything."

He laughed.

Marissa felt chill fingers of dread climb her back as Ruben smiled, pleased with himself and the situation.

"Wrong. You see, I hold all the cards. Have you forgotten you killed my poor cousin Manny? He died a terrible death, *cariño.* Bleeding out from the gut is a painful way to go."

She stammered, "You said he was fine and living in Puerto Rico."

He chuckled. "Of course I did. I couldn't very well tell the feds that his body was feeding the fish in the East Bay, now could I?" He sighed as if he were genuinely touched by sorrow for his cousin's death but then shrugged. "He died with honor. I sent a large amount of money to his mother for her loss. She understands and all is well."

"It was self-defense," she whispered, trembling. "He hit me…he was going to…" rape her. But she couldn't finish, the words were stuck in her mouth. Swallowing, she managed to protest weakly, "But I didn't mean to kill him. I was just trying to keep him away from me."

"I understand and I forgive you," Ruben said, false generosity oozing from his tone. She glared, not willing to let him think for a second she accepted his poisonous goodwill.

"You could've taken him to the hospital. He didn't have to die."

She remembered the slick slide of the knife as it plunged in Manny's stomach, blood gushing from the wound like a red, spurting fountain, spilling and staining the carpet as he fell in a heap to the floor. She could still see his wide-eyed stare, uncomprehending as he grabbed the handle protruding from his belly. And then she'd taken the baby and ran, too terrified of what she'd just done, too blind with the pain of her busted face to be fully aware of the consequences of her actions.

Ruben tsked. "Hospitals are no good. They ask questions. No, Manny died for a good cause, to protect the family. He would've wanted it that way."

"You're a heartless bastard."

"No," he disagreed easily. "I have too big a heart,

I think. See, I should kill you for what you've done. Honor demands that I snuff out that pretty light in your eyes but I can't…not yet, anyway. I have too many plans for you and I. Plans I've waited a long time to put into play. Do you know every time I made your sister squeal like a pig in heat when I was pumping into her I was thinking of you? How much I wanted to taste your body, feel you beneath me. You gave me a taste, *cariño,* but it was not enough. It would never be enough. You are mine. And if I find out anyone else has touched you, I will peel his skin from his bones. Do you hear me?"

Marissa shrank away from him, the urge to get away nearly overpowering. He caught her revulsion and his expression turned ugly. "If you don't start showing your gratitude for my kindness to you I will do something you don't like."

"You mean killing my sister and my friend Layla weren't enough? You think that's not going to stick with me for the rest of my life?" she spat.

"Your sister brought on her punishment. Nobody takes what's mine!"

"You never wanted Jenna!"

"She's mine!" he roared as if that were some kind of legitimate justification for beating Mercedes while she was pregnant, throwing her down a flight of stairs and then nearly forcibly dragging her to the abortionist when she refused to kill her own baby. "If I want to train her to be a whore just like her mother, it's my right to do so! Mercedes thought a little piece of paper would keep her safe from my wrath and her stupidity earned her a bullet. I pray you don't make the same mistake, *cariño*."

"And what of Layla? What did she do?" Marissa said, tears streaming down her face. Ruben reached over to wipe away the moisture and she jerked away.

He licked at the salty moisture on his thumb and Marissa nearly gagged. "Your friend was no longer useful. And I couldn't very well let her go. She was a mess." He shook his head regretfully. "A bloody, torn-up mess. She would've gone straight to the cops and not even my influence there would've allowed me to walk away from that. But her blood is on your hands. If you hadn't run, she'd still be alive. It's your fault, Marissa. You have blood on your hands, too."

"Let me out," she demanded, nearing hysterical tears if she didn't get away from him. "Let me out!"

"No," he answered calmly. "We have not discussed your new role."

"My new role?" she repeated, disgust in her voice. "I have no role in your life. I'd rather die."

"No, you wouldn't. You would do anything for that brat. She's my insurance policy. As long as you remain by my side, loving and attentive as any good wife should be, we will raise Jenna together. If you cross me, try to leave or anything else that doesn't please me, I will slice that baby flesh one piece at a time and make you watch as she screams. And when I'm done, I'll toss her little carcass to the dogs."

Marissa couldn't breathe. The air in the cloistered Town Car was suddenly hot and lacking oxygen. Oh, Jenna. The very idea of that happening to her beloved niece made her want to throw up. Her heart rate doubled and she feared passing out. "How could you?" she gasped, black dots dancing in front her. "She's your own daughter!"

He shrugged. "We will make many babies, *cariño*. Ones not tainted by your sister's blood." He reached over to rub her belly possessively. "You will give me sons. Or die trying."

Marissa gulped, straining to hold on to the thin thread of consciousness but for the first time in her life…she fainted.

"WE GOT ENOUGH?" Archer growled, pulling his gun to double-check his ammunition. He was ready to pound a new expression into that slick Latino scumbag, one that was minus a few teeth.

"We got him," Jeremiah said, "although you know his high-price lawyer is going to squawk about the recording without his knowledge bullshit."

"Not worried about a technicality," Archer said, gearing up in a Kevlar vest and strapping more ammunition into his tool belt.

"You should," Jeremiah warned, strapping gear, as well.

Rico entered just as they were finished. "Hot diggity. Where we headin', boys?" he asked, the shit-eating grin on his face almost comical if it weren't for the circumstances.

"We're going to catch ourselves a big fish. Want to come?" Jeremiah asked.

"You know it. I love to fish. Especially when the catch is a scum-sucking drug lord from the East Side."

Archer bared his teeth in a travesty of a smile, ready to do some damage. "Then let's do it. I'm hungry for a fight."

"Yeehaw!" Rico said, his exuberance masking the stone-cold professional that Archer knew his team-mate was. "Let's ride, amigos."

"You got a 20 on that Town Car?" Archer asked as they walked out the door.

"Yeah," Jeremiah said as he checked the GPS tracker but suddenly frowned. "Shit. We just lost signal."

Archer knew that meant one of two things and neither boded well for Marissa.

"It could be a glitch," Rico suggested, all jocularity gone. "You know that happens with the tiny wires."

"It isn't a glitch," Archer returned, not willing to give himself false hope. Somehow Ruben had figured out she was wearing a wire. Son of a—

"Arch…"

"Yeah, I know," Archer said, compressing his lips

to a tight line. "Regroup," he muttered beneath a stream of hot curse words.

"We need a team if we're going into the compound. It's not going to be as simple as walking in with a warrant. A traffic stop is one thing...taking him down on his own turf without backup...that's a suicide mission," Jeremiah said, his frown deepening, but at Archer's ominous expression he added, "We'll go in when the sun goes down. She's a smart girl. She'll figure out a way to stay alive."

Archer felt sweat beading his forehead and nausea clamping down on his gut. "I know," he said, bluffing. Perhaps if he said it enough times he'd believe it. But right about now he didn't know what kind of hell Marissa was going to have to live through until they got there.

Just stay alive, honey. Stay alive. I'm coming for you.

RUBEN CRUSHED THE TINY beadlike earrings between his fingers. Wires protruded from the thin metal casing and he knew his *cariño* had betrayed him...again.

At first he'd simply planned to take them away so he could replace them with something more beautiful than the simple gold studs, but as he plucked them from her ears while she was out cold, he realized what he was holding.

And it made him see red.

He would punish her. She needed a strong hand, someone to teach her boundaries. He ran his knuckles across her cheek. He was the man to do this and he accepted the challenge gleefully. Even now, as she slept, her beauty stirred him like no other. Her sister had been a cheap imitation of the vision in his possession.

But, even as he visually caressed her body, lingering on the soft, plump mounds of the breasts that haunted his dreams, he thought of how he was going to make her scream in pain.

His breathing accelerated and he hardened with anticipation. A woman's tears of agony were a beautiful thing, a gift that he relished wringing from their eyes as they pleaded for mercy. His thoughts wandered to Layla and he smiled at the memory of her last moment. He sighed. So nice.

Ah, *cariño*. Your tears will water my soul. Just as it should be. We will have a wonderful life together.

CHAPTER SIXTEEN

NIGHT COULDN'T COME fast enough. Archer paced until Rico finally threw a pen at him and made him stop.

"You're driving me crazy with your pacing, bro," Rico said, glowering at Archer. They were all edgy, waiting for the sun to go down so they could infiltrate the compound high in the Oakland hills. They had a full team, sixteen officers in full SWAT mode, with Rico, Jeremiah and Archer each leading a group to surround the four-thousand-square-foot residence.

"How much longer?" Archer asked Jeremiah.

"Another hour. You know the drill. Go take a powder. We won't leave without you."

Archer grunted in answer and strode from the room. He felt as if a hundred ants were crawling over his skin, as his nerves played ping-pong with one another. He never should've let her walk out the front door with that psycho. He should've found a different way rather than using her as bait but they'd needed Ruben to believe that everything was cool.

The fact that Marissa was a terrible liar weighed on his mind and almost made him discard the plan on that issue alone but he knew they likely had one shot to make this work and so they'd gone ahead with the plan. If anything happened to her... A vision of Kandy Kane's dead body flashed in his mind, only this time it was Marissa and he nearly lost what little breakfast he'd eaten.

Detouring to a secure phone, he dialed the number to the family fostering Jenna while she was in federal custody.

Rachel Forsmann, a nice but no-nonsense woman, picked up the line. "This is Rachel Forsmann. How may I help you?"

"This is Agent Brant. How is Jenna doing?" he asked, wishing he could see her. "Is she all right?"

"Code word, please," came the pleasant but firm voice on the other line, and Archer relaxed, glad to know that Forsmann was a stickler for details.

"Code word *hot dog*."

"Thank you, Agent Brant. She was a little fussy but after a hot meal she settled right down. She's a good sleeper. She conked out a little bit ago. Would you like me to wake her?"

"No. Let her sleep. I just..." wanted to hear her little voice. Better yet he wanted to hold her in his arms and tell her that everything was going to be okay and that the only mother she'd ever remember was coming home soon. But he couldn't say any of those things and not just because she was already fast asleep. "Never mind. Just take good care of her. She's a special kid."

"All children are special, Agent Brant," Rachel returned evenly. "Is there anything else you require?"

"No. I'm sorry to have bothered you."

"No trouble, Agent Brant. Perhaps…you'd like to come and see her tomorrow?" she suggested.

"Yeah…we'll see," he said, not willing to commit to anything. He didn't want to jinx the operation. His cell phone buzzed at his hip. It was Jeremiah. Time to hit it. "Good night, Mrs. Forsmann."

"Good night, Agent Brant. We'll be home all day tomorrow if you change your mind."

He replaced the office phone on the cradle and returned his cell phone to the holster on his utility belt.

"Let's rock and roll," he muttered and prepared to go to battle, to fight to the death if need be, for the woman he loved.

MARISSA AWOKE IN A luxurious room filled with crisp white linens on the king-size bed, framed high-quality prints of priceless paintings gracing the walls, and thick white Berber carpet under her feet. The carpet reminded her too much of the carpet her sister had had in her apartment when she was killed. She tucked her feet under her and rubbed at her eyes, wondering what the hell was going on. A soft knock at the door startled her and she pulled the comforter around her. The door opened without her invitation. Expecting Ruben, she grabbed the first thing her fingers could reach and prepared to hurtle the small brass alarm clock at whoever had the misfortune of walking in, but when she saw a timid Puerto Rican woman coming with fresh towels she lowered the clock and apologized.

"I thought you were someone else," she said, trying to lessen the look of trepidation in the woman's eyes. "I'm not the kind of person who throws things on a normal everyday basis," she explained, feeling like a toad for scaring the poor woman.

"Here are your towels," the woman said softly, placing them on the polished surface of the black lacquered dresser. She turned to scurry from the room but Marissa hoped she might find an ally in this timid woman and asked her name.

The woman looked confused. "I bring towels. You wash."

"I know what the towels are for. I just wondered what your name is," she said, her hopes for a friendly face in this hell dwindling quickly. "My name is—"

"You wash."

Marissa frowned. "Thank you but I'm not staying. I don't need to shower."

The woman narrowed her small eyes at Marissa and a chill returned to her spine. "You wash or he get mad."

Marissa didn't waste time playing dumb. She knew whom the maid was referring to. She swallowed. "Or what?" she challenged.

The woman shook her head and simply repeated herself. "You wash. He likes his woman clean." And then left the room.

Marissa shuddered. She was not his woman. Where was Archer? Why hadn't he come for her yet? She jumped from the bed and grabbed her shoes, slipping them on as quickly as possible. For reassurance, she touched her ears where the studs were and froze when her fingers found nothing but the soft pierced flesh of her earlobe. "Oh, God," she squeaked, dropping to her knees to search the thick carpet, threading her fingers through the strands in the hopes of finding them before Ruben did but she came up empty. Panic distracted her to the point she didn't realize the door had reopened until a small whine of the hinges made her say over her shoulder, "I don't need to wash!" when she thought the woman had returned.

But it wasn't the small woman.

"Looking for something?"

Marissa stilled and rose slowly to turn and face Ruben. "As a matter of fact I lost a pair of earrings. Gold studs. They were quite special to me."

"A shame. I will replace them."

"I don't want anything from you."

"Not even, perhaps, mercy?"

"Mercy?" she repeated, disgust curling her lip. "When have you ever given anything as generous as mercy to another human being. You're not capable."

A slow smile twisted his face. "You know me so well. Another reason we are well-suited."

"Go screw yourself, Ruben."

Ruben snapped his fingers and two of his thugs appeared. They looked much like Manny did before she gutted him, like gorillas stuffed in ill-fitting suits. "Bring her," he instructed and they advanced toward her.

"Don't touch me," she warned them but they weren't inclined to listen. She tried to run but they were quick in spite of their luggish appearance. She let loose with a hearty screech that surely alerted the neighbors that something terrible was going on but no sound of sirens followed as they half dragged, half pulled her behind their boss.

"Where are you taking me?" she ground out, glaring at the back of Ruben's head.

"To what will become—in time—your favorite place. It's already mine."

Somehow she didn't think he was taking her to Starbucks.

Ruben opened double doors leading to a room that made her jaw drop and her feet seek purchase against the hardwood floor of the hallway.

Oh, God. Her next thought was suffused within a

terrified scream as the doors closed behind them and locks slid into place. Archer…please save me.

ARCHER'S ADRENALINE WAS pumping, awakening every sense as the team went into their positions around the perimeter of the house Ruben called his compound.

The guards were easy enough to dispatch, knocking them out with tranq darts that would give them a helluva headache when they came to but would leave no lasting effects. Not that Archer wouldn't mind leaving behind a swath of dead bodies in his current frame of mind but Jeremiah made him promise he would use the tranqs and not the Glock so he didn't have to deal with the paperwork that the General would foist on him when the assignment was over.

They managed to procure a detailed floor plan of the building from city hall but it was anyone's guess where Ruben was keeping Marissa. The key would be to get inside before alerting any of the interior guards so they could ascertain where she was being held.

A scream—muffled but still audible—floated into the night and Archer stiffened, knowing it was Marissa. Every hair on his body stood on end at the tortured sound.

But he held his position.

They crept along the side wall, aiming for the kitchen door. Archer gained access quickly and easily without making a sound. Silently padding across the tiled floor, they subdued a Puerto Rican woman and two more thugs.

But they didn't see the third in time before he sounded the alarm. Suddenly gunfire erupted and Archer had to find cover. He ducked behind a wall and returned fire, dropping the man who had first took a shot at them. His team rushed in formation to take down the men who were running and firing off wild shots in the hopes that they might hit something. Bullets whizzed by and lodged themselves with a spray of plaster into the walls. Men screamed as the bullets that didn't land harmlessly ripped into flesh.

"We're going to need EMS for these scum-suckers," Archer said into his walkie and kept moving. He was single-minded in his focus. If it shot at him, he shot back. It was a pretty simple plan. And so far it was working.

Since stealth was no longer an issue, he kicked in the right side of a set of double doors, rifle at the ready.

But if he lived to be a hundred...he'd never be ready for what was waiting for him in that room.

Marissa. Arms above her head, hung like a side of beef, she twisted, naked and bruised, blood trickling down the side of her mouth, while wheals of red-dened flesh puckered in angry lines across her back. His eyes stung as he blinked back tears of agony but he waited for the all clear from his team that Ruben was not hiding elsewhere in the room. He could hear Jeremiah and Rico on the radio. House was secure. No sign of Ruben Ortiz.

"What's your 20, Arch?" Rico asked, amid the scratch of static on the radio.

"Bedroom on the south end of the house, past the kitchen," he answered hoarsely, holstering his gun and going to Marissa. His hands trembled as he went to get her down. "Get a medic. Immediately."

He wasn't even sure if she was still alive. Her face was swollen. Her lip split, both eyes blackened, and finger marks encircled her neck as if Ruben had tried strangling her but then changed his mind and moved to a different mode of torture. She was damn near unrecognizable.

Someone handed him a fine linen sheet they'd ripped from the bed to wrap her in. They helped him in silence as he cut her down and then gently wrapped her battered body with loving and tender attention. She whimpered but the sound was so weak, he wasn't sure he heard it.

"Where's the goddamn medic!" Tears blurred his vision and he prayed like a man who knew he was going to hell and it was his last day on Earth. He prayed for a miracle.

CHAPTER SEVENTEEN

MARISSA FLOATED WITH the weightlessness of water yet she wasn't wet. She heard Jenna's sweet laughter but couldn't find her hiding spot. She felt Archer's touch but when she reached out to touch him, he disappeared.

Come back, she wanted to shout but her vocal cords were paralyzed. Her mouth worked but no sound came out. Panic caused her heart to flutter like a trapped bird.

Archer, she wanted to cry out. Archer, where are you?

Ruben's face appeared before her and she shrank back. He'd done terrible things to her. So much pain. It hurt so bad she couldn't hold back any longer. She'd tried to remain stoic, to laugh in the face of his efforts but the pain had been excruciating and she'd buckled under its weight. She'd thought Archer would save her. Why didn't he?

The first thing Marissa became fully aware of was moisture making a slow trail from the corners of her eyes. Then came the steady beep of machines, the scratch of utilitarian sheets and the hard surface of the bed she was lying in.

Her body shrieked in protest when she turned her head to focus. The world was blurry but she knew she was in a hospital. Fear snaked its way into her heart as she wondered if Ruben was still there, seeing to her welfare after nearly killing her, just so he could do it to her all over again. She moaned as the pain hit a glorious crescendo and she heard the deep, low rumble of a man's voice that immediately soothed her even as he seemed gruff with the other person in the room. Suddenly, the pain floated away like a balloon on a hot summer day, heading for the freedom of the clouds. And she sank into a blissful sleep that was dark, quiet and safe.

ARCHER RUBBED AT THE GRIT in his eyes, afraid to catch even a moment's rest while Marissa remained in intensive care. It'd been two days since he found her at the compound; two days since she fell into a coma.

Jeremiah and Rico entered the room. Rico handed him a cup of black coffee. He grunted his appreciation. It was his fourth cup already.

"How's she doing today?" Jeremiah asked, his tone grave. "Any change?"

Archer cleared his throat, feeling as if spiders had taken up residence in his trachea, and tried to repeat what the doctor had told him. "She's stable but that bastard beat her pretty good. Broke a few ribs and the orbital bone above her left cheek." His voice broke and both men gave him the courtesy of not mentioning it as he tried to continue but going down a laundry list of the injuries sustained by the woman he loved more than life itself wasn't quite so easy. "Doc says when her mind is ready, she'll come out of the coma."

Jeremiah shook his head. "Sick piece of shit," he muttered, promising, "we'll catch him."

Rico agreed, looking as bothered as Jeremiah by the turn of events. Archer imagined the paperwork involved but couldn't muster the appropriate response. Technically, this was his detail. He ought to be the one to file the lengthy reports, seeing as four thugs had ended up dying that night—none of whom were Ruben.

"Any leads on where he might be holed up?" Archer asked, swallowing a mouthful of substandard coffee that was probably dirt in another life, yet grateful for the caffeine kick even if his burned out receptors were barely functioning at this point. "What about that club of his?"

"We checked. Served a warrant to search the premises this morning. He wasn't there and no one is talking," Rico said.

"Why would they? He's got them scared for their lives and rightly so. The bastard wouldn't think twice of gutting any one of them if they talked," Archer said, rubbing the bridge of his nose as a yawn cracked his jaw. "What about family? Mother? Father? Brother? Someone's got to be related to that asshole. As much as I'd like to believe he crawled out from underneath a rock somewhere, he started off with family. Maybe if we find them…we can squeeze them a little for a change. Give him a taste of his own medicine."

"Any ideas what name I should look for? We already checked under Ortiz and came up with nothing," Jeremiah said, his expression grim.

"What does he pay taxes under?" Archer asked.

"Ortiz. That's the name on his social, too, but I can't seem to dig up a corresponding birth certificate with that name."

"What about his juvenile record?"

"Ortiz," Jeremiah answered, indicating he'd already tried searching there but came up empty.

Archer's brain was sluggish and he hated being so weak when it was crucial that he remain sharp. He gave himself a shake and focused. He thought of Marissa. It was likely she knew if he went by another name but she wasn't able to help them. Mercedes would've known but she was dead. It took him a minute to get there but suddenly a light in his head that started off rather dim began to glow like a beacon of hope. "Jenna's birth certificate. Mercedes would've listed Ruben as the father. It's possible she might've written down an alias rather than the name he's become notorious for to protect her daughter."

"I'm on it," Rico declared. "This could be the piece of the puzzle that we need. I'll keep you posted. If I find out anything, you'll be the first call. Oh, and one more thing, we flushed out the cop that was on the take. Too damn easy and not a lot of fun to squeeze. He squealed the minute we took him into custody. He also ratted out a low-level sergeant, too. All in all, not very satisfying but at least they're paying for their bad judgment."

Archer nodded his thanks, glad to hear the news but too bone-weary to ask for details. He'd get those later. Jeremiah was an artist when it came to interrogation. He could imagine Jeremiah's disappointment when the dirty cop caved before he could truly work his magic on the guy. Archer rubbed his face, then noted that Jeremiah appeared pensive as if something were weighing heavily on his mind. Archer didn't have the energy to waste time pussyfooting around so he just asked. "What's eating you?"

Jeremiah sighed, his stare resting on Marissa's still figure in the hospital bed, and Archer couldn't tell where the man's thoughts were wandering. "Listen, Arch, we have to talk," he finally said.

"This can't wait?" Archer asked, somehow knowing this conversation had been coming, probably since before the situation with Marissa. The past three years had been rough. Not just on the job but personally. In a way he welcomed this conversation. It would force him to deal with the things he'd been putting off for a long time.

"It can but not long. The General wants you to reevaluate your commitment to the team."

He expected it, saw it coming even, but when it was put in his face, he bristled. "My commitment? I didn't realize my commitment was ever an issue. In fact, for the past three years my life has been the job. How can a person get more committed than that?"

"It's not that and you know it. You're a good agent. Fierce, determined and fearless. Just the kind of guy we like on the team but your heart left a long time ago." Jeremiah let that sink in. And it did.

Archer let his gaze stray to Marissa and he couldn't deny what Jeremiah was saying. His heart had left. It went with the woman he was praying over as he stood silently waiting for her to open her eyes. He absently smoothed the coarse blanket thermal over her bottom half and wondered if he ought to bring a softer blanket from home.

"If she doesn't make it…"

"She will. She's strong."

"It's my fault she's lying here. We never should've used a civilian for a job like this."

"No. It's Ruben Ortiz's fault," Jeremiah corrected him. "And he's going to pay for what he's done to her and so many others. We got him. And we'll find him.

It's what we do. But in the meantime, take a moment for yourself and really think about what you want. Your life doesn't have to be all about the job. It never did. That was your choice. And I think you've been paying for that choice for a long time."

"What else do I have?" Archer asked, his tone mocking. Hell, he knew Jeremiah was giving him some solid advice but right now he was too damn messed up to hear the entire message. He didn't want to hear it. "I've got the job and the job's got me. Period. I'm not cut out for backyard barbecues and birthday parties. Do you think I can just flip a switch and suddenly become a family man like she wants? Like she deserves?" The last part came out sounding desperate and he couldn't hold Jeremiah's knowing stare. There was no judgment there, just friendship, yet Archer felt he was being picked apart from all directions. "Why don't you tell the General that if he wants to fire me then he knows all the right paperwork he has to file. Until then, back off. I'm not going anywhere."

"Don't make this personal," Jeremiah said, exasperated.

"Is there any other way to take it when you've been politely asked to quietly get the hell out? Oh, sure, you wrapped it real nice in some bullshit packaging about my heart not being in the job any longer but we both know what this is really about. Kandy. And now Marissa. Two screwups in rapid succession

KIMBERLY VAN METER 213

of each other. I get it. And if you think that I don't want to have a redo every single day for both of these women you're sadly mistaken. But suggesting that I call it quits is just insulting after all the time I've put in with this agency."

"No one's asking you to quit, you hotheaded jackass," Jeremiah retorted in a dangerous tone, his eyes flashing with all the pissed-off ire of a man pushed to the edge of reason. "If you'd shut up a minute and just listen to what I'm saying, you'd realize I'm right and you're being a dick. You want to throw away your life, content to wallow in self-imposed misery and teenage-girl angst, go right ahead, but don't try and blame others for when you're determined to keep your head stuck up your ass."

Archer and Jeremiah stared each other down, two men who were equally matched in strength and brawn but at the moment Archer knew Jeremiah had him beat in the brain department. He also knew Jeremiah had called him on his pity-party and there was nothing he could do but just take his licks. He didn't have to like it, though. "You done?" he asked, sour and still pissed-off but moderately chastised.

"Just about," Jeremiah stated. "You've got paper-work to file. Don't forget. This ain't high school and I ain't your girlfriend. So, file your own damn report."

"It'll be on the General's desk by morning," Archer said and Jeremiah responded with a curt nod before turning to leave. Just as he reached the threshold, Archer offered the man what he should've given him a long time ago. "Thanks, man," he said softly. "I owe you."

Jeremiah paused but didn't turn. "You don't owe me anything. We've all been where you're at sometime in our lives. Why else would we be in this job?"

Archer nodded and nothing more was said between them. There wasn't a need.

MARISSA FOUGHT TO OPEN her eyes but it was slow work. There was mud weighing them down and it seemed they weren't functioning properly. But she wouldn't give up. She was tired of this dark place where she floated on a breeze she couldn't feel and her mind became increasingly foggy with the details of her life. There was someone precious she needed to return to, someone who needed her in equal measure, yet she couldn't picture the person's face or remember their name. Frustration welled in mild spurts—it took too much effort to call more energy than the most basic requirement—and she tried harder to focus. But focusing brought sharp pain and that caused her to retreat, desperate to evade the agony parading up and down her body without mercy. Except this time, she faced the pain head-on, baring her teeth against the barrage of sensation searing along nerve endings and burrowing into bruised flesh. Bits of memory rushed to her mind and she cringed, once again tempted to run away but somehow she sensed that if she continued to hide, she might never return to what she'd known before. And so she fought through the mud, the agony, the memory and the temptation to hide, to finally open her eyes and keep them open.

Her vision, blurred and unfocused, tried to distinguish the shapes in the room. She could make out machines, a window, a television in the corner. And then, curled in a pink convertible chair, one that went from a recliner to an uncomfortable bed, a man sprawled snoring lightly. She blinked slowly, still trying to make sense of her world and her place in it. He was too big for that chair, she thought muzzily. He'd probably suffer a stiff neck when he woke. And then as the bits of memory came together more quickly like pieces of a puzzle snapping together she knew the man's name and it fell from her lips in a hoarse whisper.

But it fell on deaf ears. Archer was dead to the world. She closed her eyes and slept, only this time, she refused to let herself return to that dark place. This time, when she slept, it was simply that—sleep.

CHAPTER EIGHTEEN

IT WAS LATER THAT afternoon that Marissa finally truly awoke. Archer was thumbing through a magazine, not quite seeing the words nor caring for the pictures, just doing it for the sake of doing something before he lost his mind, and he realized she was stirring. The doctor had told him about involuntary movements but there was something about the sound of her movements that told him they were done with a conscious mind. Perhaps it was the breathy moan of pain or the slow slide of her legs under the blanket as she switched position for the first time without the benefit of a nurse doing manual exercises to avoid bedsores. But when he lowered the magazine, he caught the slow flutter of her eyelids and nearly wept.

He rose on shaky legs, not even realizing the magazine had dropped from his fingers, and came to her bedside. He couldn't speak. He'd imagined what this moment would feel like and all the things that he would say to her—how much he loved her, how devastated he'd been that she'd been hurt, how sorry he was for putting her in danger—but as he stared into those brown eyes he'd come to treasure above all things, all he could do was drink in the sight of her.

He wasn't sure if she saw him clearly, there was still a slightly dazed quality to her scrutiny, and when she blinked the action was slow and labored as if it took a great amount of energy to accomplish so small a task.

Her gaze roved his face, resting on the bridge of his nose, the cleft of his chin, the scruff on his jaw, and then returned to his eyes, and he felt himself falling into the rich, dark chocolate pools of her eyes.

A grief so raw and bereft replaced the pain he read there and he wondered with trepidation where in her mind she had retreated to and what she'd come back with.

And as the grief rolled into another emotion he felt the tide turning against him. Without words she asked him, "Why didn't you come for me?" and he wanted to explain how he'd tried to find her but he'd been hamstrung by correct procedure…that he wasn't John Wayne and he couldn't do as he desperately desired, which was to ride in guns-blazing to rescue her. The reproach in her eyes mingled with the glaze of pain that coated her stare as her eyelids fluttered closed and she slowly turned away from him.

The breath hitched in his chest and he struggled to keep the tears from spilling. She was right. He had no right to hope that she'd accept his excuses for why he hadn't prevented her from being assaulted or why he'd agreed to use her as bait. None of it mattered.

The nurse entered, a worried frown on her face. "I heard the monitor go off. Is she awake?" she asked him as he backed away.

"She's in pain. See that she isn't hurting," he said just as a tear escaped and ran down his cheek. And then he split. She was in good hands. She didn't need him any longer.

MARISSA HADN'T NEEDED to see Archer leave her room to know he was gone. Her mind was numb but her body was alive with knives of misery piercing her battered flesh until the nurse put in a Demerol drip following the doctor's examination. She'd suffered in silence as he shined light in her eyes, checked her vitals, questioned her to determine her mental acuity, and finally determined it was safe for her to rest.

Apparently, there was a chance for a relapse in coma patients but since her coma seemed to be caused by the trauma her body suffered, the doctor felt she was a low risk. Still, a nurse checked her every hour, popping her head into the room to ensure she was still in the here and now instead of floating off into her head.

Seeing Archer by her bedside, clothes rumpled as if he'd slept in them for days and a haunted look in his eyes ringed by fatigue, she knew he'd never left. Her gaze wandered to the pink chair in the corner and knew that was where he'd slept. She imagined him forcing down hospital food and chugging coffee.

Yet, even as the knowledge soothed her, a part—likely the part that was ravaged and beaten—demanded to know why it all had happened.

She'd known such relief the moment Archer had pressed those tiny studs into her palm and realized she wasn't alone. Her confidence had given her courage until the point she knew—right about when Ruben took a five-barbed whip to her bare back—that Archer wasn't coming for her. Her courage melted like ice cream in the hot sun and she was left with pure, unadulterated fear. She stank of it. And when she couldn't see out of either eye and her back wept blood, she'd finally broken down and begged for Ruben to stop but he was in a frenzy, his labored breathing sounding like a man in the throes of an orgasm, and she gagged on her own vomit.

Marissa closed her eyes against the horrid memory of that night and wondered if she'd ever be free of the stain.

"MARISSA'S AWAKE. I WANT a guard posted at her door," Archer said, going into Jeremiah's office. "I don't want to take any chances. Ortiz might have an informant in the hospital to tip him off if she wakes up." He was probably feeling pretty safe with Marissa still in a coma because comatose patients didn't make good witnesses on the stand but with her coming around…well, Archer wouldn't put it past the man to try and tip the scale in his favor.

"How's she doing?" Jeremiah asked.

Archer swallowed, still seeing that haunted, wounded expression in her eyes as she looked at him. "Not a doctor but she seems to be doing all right."

Jeremiah knew better than to press and moved on. "We've got a lead on your guy." This served to perk Archer up a bit. Jeremiah pulled a folder and removed the copy of a birth certificate. "You were right. Mercedes named the father of her baby as one Ruben Sandoval. Rico did some checking around and it just so happens Ruben Sandoval owns a modest home in Richmond." He double-checked a slip of paper on his desk, adding, "You up for a drive to 1414 Jubilee Court?"

Archer turned on his heel and said over his shoulder. "I'll be in the car."

JEREMIAH AND ARCHER eyeballed the humble three-bedroom bungalow located in the Larkwood Estates subdivision and noted the pretty flower boxes hanging on the front windows and the sound of children playing in their yards. It was the picture of suburbia.

"Why would Ortiz hide out here?" Archer wondered, scanning the area for anything that appeared suspicious or out of the ordinary aside from the two federal agents sitting in their car in the neighborhood. "This is a far cry from the compound. You'd think his hideout would be something more like the one he lived in."

"Unless he bought this place for someone else. Like his mother," Jeremiah suggested as they exited the car. He grinned at Archer. "Let's go see if Mama's boy is visiting."

"With pleasure," Archer growled.

"Oh, and try not to shoot anyone. There are kids all over this place," Jeremiah said under his breath as they ascended the three short steps to the front door. A Bless All Who Enter plaque hung from a nail and white lace curtains covered the side window.

Archer rapped twice on the door and while he waited he scanned the yard, the house, everything within his range, watching for sudden movement, anything that might signal that Ortiz was on the run.

Just as Archer went to knock again, the door opened and a small Mexican woman, probably no taller than Archer's chest, appeared.

Her welcoming smile disappeared when Archer and Jeremiah flashed their identification. "Hello, Mrs. Sandoval, we're looking for your son, Ruben Ortiz. Is he here by any chance?" Jeremiah asked.

"No," she answered and tried to shut the door but Archer was faster than and slid his foot between the door and the jamb. She glared at him and then drew the door back and slammed it on his foot. Holy hell that hurt.

Archer swore and gritted his teeth against the pain. "Not so fast, Granny," he muttered and pushed the door open with one quick and hard motion that sent her stumbling back.

"You can't come in here without a warrant," she screeched, fists balled and ready to take a swing at either of them by the look on her face.

"I see where Ortiz gets his sunny disposition," Archer remarked, moving past her in spite of her protests. "Where is he? Save us the time of ripping this cozy place apart and just tell us where that scum-sucking son of yours is hiding."

"Go to hell."

Archer chuckled. "Nice."

Jeremiah produced the warrant and waved it in front of her. "Here's your warrant. And you're under arrest for assaulting a federal agent. Hands behind your back, ma'am," he said as she stared at him in disbelief.

"My son will make you pay for this insult," she declared even as Jeremiah pulled her birdlike appendages behind her back to handcuff.

Archer looked at her dispassionately. "Yeah? I look forward to it. Now where is he?"

Her mouth tightened and her eyes narrowed but she said nothing. Oh, so that's how it is, Archer thought, looking to Jeremiah. "I'll take the bedrooms. Did you bring your sledgehammer?"

"It's in the car."

"Don't you dare," she said, indignant at the thought of her home being trashed in such a way.

Archer glanced at the orderly way of everything from the dust-free knickknacks to the pristine white carpet, and he grinned in a way that told her he'd enjoy every minute. "Oh, I dare," he said easily. "And it's perfectly legal. With reasonable doubt I can tear down every wall, climb into your attic and pull the guts out of your insulation to see what's hiding in there because I believe you're harboring a man wanted by the federal government on charges of rape, sodomy, felony assault and drug trafficking. And those are just the violent offenses. Our sister branch of the government, also known as the IRS, wants to conduct an audit of his business practices now that they know he operates under an alias as well as his legal name. Another thing, if you're harboring a fugitive…that's a crime, too. So, are you willing to go down for this piece of crap?"

Apparently, she was. The old woman was buttoned up tighter than a drum. Fine. "Keep her here. I want her to see this," he instructed Jeremiah before striding from the house to go get the sledgehammer. He returned moments later and hefted it in his hand. "Let's start with the master bedroom. Better make sure there are no false walls," he said with affected cheerfulness. In truth he was raging pissed-off, hating that Ortiz could get anyone to remain loyal out of choice. Sure, it was the woman who spawned him but still…if she could support him even after hearing what a monster he was, that put her down as equally bad in his book.

Archer went into the first bedroom. It was made up for a guest but it looked as if no one had slept there in months. He went to the closet and jerked the doors open. He knocked on the walls. "Sounds hollow to me," he declared loudly and then swung the sledge-hammer, burying it in the plaster handle-deep. "Better give it another whack, just to be sure," he called out, grinning when he heard the old woman start to cuss him out in Spanish. "Here we go," he said, relishing the feel of the blunt tool smashing into the wall, imagining it was Ruben's head as it took down the drywall in great chunks.

He poked his head out. "Nothing there. I'll check the master bedroom."

"You bastard!" she shrieked, eliciting a wider grin on Archer's part. He glanced around the room and spied a series of porcelain figures on the dresser. They were obviously placed there with great care and prized since they were not in the living room where they might get jostled or touched by visitors. He picked up one indiscriminately and then let it slip from his fingers to smash into a thousand pieces on the hardwood floor. "Sorry about that," he called out. "Hope it wasn't valuable. But these things happen you know. I hope nothing else gets broken…."

Expecting more shrieking, perhaps more colorful

language thrown at him in a different language, but instead Jeremiah's voice reached him.

"Archer. We've got a situation." His voice was relaxed but there was a note of urgency underlying the deceptive calm that quickly told Archer Ruben was probably in the house.

"Yeah, be there in a minute," he answered, gently setting the sledgehammer down and pulling his gun. He came around the corner, back against the wall and found Ruben with a gun to Jeremiah's head.

"The man's quieter than the wind," Jeremiah said by way of explanation, shrugging with his hands up. The old woman stood by her son, a triumphant gleam in her sharp eyes that made Archer want to break a few more knickknacks.

"You've caused me so much trouble," Ruben stated matter-of-factly but there was rage in his voice. "First my home and my woman…that I could've forgiven and let bygones be bygones but you've taken things too far, *federales,* coming here and terrorizing my mama. One might question your upbringing."

Archer shrugged. "The same could be said for you."

"My boy is a good man," the woman snapped and Ortiz silenced her with a look. She quieted under her son's authority and Archer realized the cultural differences at work. Ortiz was the man of the house. She'd do whatever he required of her, even if that meant going down protecting him. Archer wanted to shake some sense into the old woman but by the looks of it, it was too late for her. She likely would've let him tear her house asunder to protect her son. But Ortiz on the other hand didn't like his personal possessions messed with, and it had probably driven him crazy to know Archer was destroying everything with gleeful abandon.

A twisted smile formed on his mouth. It was small retribution but he'd take anything he could get at this moment.

"What's so funny?" Ortiz demanded. He pressed the gun harder against Jeremiah's temple. "I'm about to blow your friend's brains out and you think this is funny?" he said, his voice dropping dangerously. His gaze never left Archer's as he directed his mother to get some trash bags. "You've already made a big enough mess," he said in explanation.

"Oh, I see. You're planning to kill us, bury our bodies and then go on your merry way? Business as usual I suspect by looking at your track record," Archer surmised, deadly calm in spite of the circumstances. This wasn't the first time he'd had a gun in his face or his partner's. He was getting tired of it, though. "Good plan. The only problem? We've got about fifty agents on their way right now. You think we'd come here without backup? You're not only insane but stupid."

"Without a body they've got nothing on me,"

Ruben sneered. "I know how the law works, my friend."

"Oh, I know you do. You've spent your life evading it with every loophole available to you. Except this time there are no loopholes for you to squeeze through. We've got you, Ortiz. We've got you so good, the only deal your lawyer is going to be able to push is life in prison without possibility of parole over the death penalty."

Ruben looked uncertain and Jeremiah must've felt the slightest change in the pressure against his temple for he reacted with lightning speed, throwing his elbow straight into Ortiz's gut and then connecting with the man's nose as he fell forward gasping for air. The gun went flying and the shrewish old woman ran forward with claws outstretched in spite of her man-acled hands. Archer simply put his foot in her path, sending her sprawling.

"My hip," she howled, rolling on the floor, and Archer stepped over her to where Ortiz lay curled on the floor, moaning about police brutality and a lawsuit. "You broke my hip, you bastard!"

Archer ignored the hag's screeching and stared down at Ortiz. Then he slowly lifted the man from his position on the floor to his feet while Jeremiah retrieved Ortiz's gun.

Ortiz grinned, blood staining his teeth as it leaked from his broken nose. "Do your worst, *federales*," he said. "I own this town. I'll walk and every day you'll have to look over your shoulder because I'll be there, watching and waiting, to have my revenge. No one takes what is mine."

Jeremiah took the old lady to put her in the back of the car and gave Archer a knowing look. "Just put him in cuffs. We'll deal with the rest later," he said and walked to the car with the old woman, who was limping and crying about her hip.

"That's right, lawman, cuff me so we can get this over with," Ortiz taunted as Archer jerked him around to clamp the cuffs on his wrists. He thought of Marissa and how she already feared that this man would do exactly that—stalk her and the baby until he got what he wanted—and then pictured Marissa's slack body as she'd hung like an animal on a hook in that bedroom, and then her friend Layla and how Ortiz had brutalized her before snuffing out her life. He realized the justice system might just let him go and he couldn't take that chance. He slowly let Ruben's hands go.

"What are you doing?" the man demanded, turning to stare at Archer. "Cuff me. Follow your procedure like a good little *federale*. I want to get this over with. I have plans for this evening to visit a friend in the hospital."

It was the leer that pushed him over the edge. Archer grinned like a madman. "Run, you piece of shit," he said softly.

Ruben blinked. "What?"

"You heard me. I said run."

"No." He shook his head, putting his hands out. "I want to be cuffed."

"No? What happened to the big man? The man who likes to terrorize women?" Archer mocked.

Real fear started to cloud the man's stare as he realized what Archer was doing and he shook his head vehemently. "Cuff me!" he fairly shrieked and Archer's grin widened. "You can't do this. I have rights! I'm an unarmed man!"

"How I see it, you rushed me for my gun and in the struggle my gun went off and you were mortally wounded." Archer relished the man's fear. Ruben started to look nervously for help but Archer knew Jeremiah would wait. They both knew the score and how it had to end. He gestured to Ruben with his gun and said, "C'mon on, now, make it look good. I'll even let you get in a good hit before I blow your sorry ass to kingdom come you son of a bitch."

"You can't do this," he whimpered, his eyes flitting back and forth and spit gathering at the corners of his lips. "You're a cop…you'll go to prison for this."

"Some things are worth it," Archer said with a shrug, and then he narrowed his stare and growled. "Now, I said *run*."

JEREMIAH HEARD THE SHOT and he closed his eyes briefly. The woman in the back of the car stopped moaning and turned scared eyes to the house. When

Archer emerged alone and gestured to him, she started to wail.

He jogged back to the house and followed Archer to the dead body of Ruben Ortiz. "What happened?" he asked, although he already knew.

"He went for my gun. There was a struggle. He died," Archer said flatly.

"God, the paperwork." Jeremiah sighed, pinching the bridge of his nose. He radioed for the ambulance then looked at Archer, who didn't seem the least bit remorseful for shooting a man in cold blood. He knew not every case came together neat and tidy, and loose ends got people killed. Losing Ruben Ortiz was not a tragedy but losing Archer would be. He looked at his friend and hoped Archer saw understanding in his eyes for what would come next would not be easy but Jeremiah would stand by him.

CHAPTER NINETEEN

MARISSA WAS RELEASED from the hospital and took a cab to her apartment. Muscles stiff from so much inactivity and her injuries, she moved slowly up the stairs to a life that seemed unreal. She opened the door to chaos, too numb to care that her home was trashed, and simply closed the door and waded through the wreckage to her bedroom.

There it was just as bad but she pushed away the debris of broken things and clothes strewn about and climbed into the familiar feel of her queen-size bed. Crawling under the comforter, she wanted to stay there until she died, unable to think beyond the moment, unable to see past the trauma she'd lived through.

Several hours later she awoke and realized she couldn't let herself slide into nothingness. Rising stiffly, she left the bedroom and started to clean as best she could. Jenna was with a foster family for the time being but that had to change as soon as possible. She didn't know how she would make that happen but she'd find a way. She still had her nest egg, perhaps they would move far away. Perhaps. She felt worn down by the situation but just as she nearly succumbed to the despair creeping along the edges, looking for an opening in her mental wall, she heard a short knock at the door. Fear made her freeze until Archer's voice on the other side made her realize it was okay.

She unlatched the door and opened it, gasping when she saw Jenna in his arms. The baby went instantly to her and she cried in pain and joy as the toddler gave her sweet, sloppy kisses all over her face.

"May I come in?" he asked, a short smile at the reunion. She nodded and stepped aside, careful to avoid the shattered mess of her end table she'd yet to wrestle into a trash bag. He eyed the mess and frowned. "You can't live here."

"It's my home," she said in answer, too overjoyed with having Jenna safe and in her arms to fight with him on the subject. She sat on the sofa raining kisses on Jenna's crown and finally had the guts to look at Archer. He appeared as haggard and worn as she, something was eating at his soul, and she suspected it had everything to do with the news he had come to share. She quieted, fear in her heart making her stomach clench. "Is she going back to him?" she asked.

At that he shook his head and relief was sudden

and sharp. "Thank God," she breathed. "Is he going to prison for what he did to me and Layla?"

He shook his head again, resulting in confusion. "I don't understand," she said, frowning. "What's going on?"

"He's dead."

"Dead?"

He nodded, and suddenly she knew. "You killed him."

"There was a struggle. He went for my gun. I shot him in self-defense," he answered, almost by rote, and Marissa knew by the hard look in Archer's eyes that he was lying. She looked away, not wanting that knowledge even if it meant she and Jenna were safe and could move on with their lives. "You don't have to worry about him coming after you or Jenna. With a recommendation from our office, the courts agreed that the best place for Jenna was with you. You're free to return to your life as it was before."

She slanted a look at him. Her life would never be the same. Ever. She felt broken inside. Still, she nodded numbly.

Silence filled the gap between them and Marissa knew she should thank him for all he'd done for her. It wasn't that gratitude wasn't in her heart because it was, but so much remained between them that she didn't trust herself to open her mouth and just say "thank you."

There was a part of her that wanted to throw

herself into his arms and beg him to take her away from the ghosts of her recent past but a stronger part of herself remained tightly contained, questioning why he hadn't saved her when it mattered the most and how he could've killed a man in cold blood. She expected that from Ruben but not from Archer, whom she considered to be the best of men.

And so she simply nodded and tightened her hold on Jenna for fear of breaking down in front of him.

"Marissa—" His expression was as choked as his voice and she shied away from the pain there. "I—"

"Please don't," she whispered. "I can't."

He nodded, understanding but not really because if he could catch a glimpse of the turmoil in her heart, ripping her apart, he'd know that she needed his strength even if she tried to refuse. But she read guilt in his body language and knew he wouldn't push her.

He came toward her and she thought he might kiss her goodbye and actually swayed in his direction but his affection was for Jenna. He caressed her head and one callused finger played with an errant curl. "Take care, kid. I expect great things from you. If you're anything like your aunt, you'll be fine."

He locked eyes with her and her throat constricted as tears welled. She thanked him with her heart and watched him walk out of her life. Again. Her mother's voice echoed in her mind from memory as she'd said to a sad fourteen-year-old girl, "Some things are not meant to be, *mija,* no matter how hard we wish them to."

But Mama, I wish so terribly much that the wishing is tearing me in two.

Her mother's voice was silent. As were Marissa's tears.

TODAY ARCHER WAS TURNING in his badge and gun. He expected to feel something other than the emptiness in his chest but there was nothing. Perhaps that was a blessing.

The General—they called him that because much like each member of his special team, his background was rooted in the military and the nickname suited him well—sat behind a wide, cherrywood desk, his round, jowled face implacable while Jeremiah stood near the federal law library lining the wall. Both men looked unhappy as hell to be there.

"Sit down," the General barked and Archer slid into a seat opposite the man who'd been his boss for the past ten years. The man who'd hand-plucked him out of the marines for this very special branch of the FBI. "This is bullshit," he declared, shooting a look at Jeremiah who simply lifted his shoulders in a flip shrug as if to say, *You try talking sense into the man. I'm done.*

"I've made my decision," Archer said, unmoved by the General's bluster or gathering frown. "You knew this was coming. I'm a loose cannon and a danger to the team. It's been a good run but it's over for me."

The General harrumphed. "Stop being such a girl. So you shot someone. Not the first time, won't be the last. It's not like you gunned down a pack of school-kids, Brant. Get your shit straight and we'll put this behind us. The best thing for you is to get back to work. I made a mistake in listening to that quack doctor who sidelined you for the past month. You're a highly trained agent who needs the adrenaline to stay fresh and tight." He paused and pulled a file. "I have the perfect assignment for you right here. Nothing too stressful, just your routine Aryan Nation flush in Kentucky. I know how you love those skin-heads. Figured it might be a nice change. I could have you out of here on the morrow. Just say the word."

Archer caught Jeremiah's look and for a brief moment he considered the offer to get away, to lose himself in the job just as he always did, but he knew Jeremiah had been right all along. His heart had left the job a long time ago and he couldn't pretend any longer that it hadn't.

"It's been an honor to serve on your team, General," Archer said, carefully placing his badge and his gun on the table. He unhooked his ID badge with special clearance and dropped it beside his gear.

"So that's it?" the General asked, resignation in his tone.

Archer's mouth twisted in a short smile. "That's it."

The General closed the file and nodded to Jeremiah. "Well, then. Agent Hawker, will you please escort Mr. Brant out of the building?"

"Yes, sir," Jeremiah said, and then he and his friend and partner made a final walk down the halls together as comrades and peers.

Rico appeared in the doorway of his office, his expression solemn. He gave Archer a stiff salute and Archer reciprocated.

The next time he saw these guys he'd be a civilian.

That is, if he ever saw them again.

Ah, there it is, he noted…sadness. Sharp and bittersweet. Yet he kept walking.

WEEKS HAD FLOWN BY AND Marissa had settled into a routine that included returning to work, replacing her broken furniture and finding a day care for Jenna that was near her employment. Since the state had awarded custody of Jenna to Marissa, she had started receiving a stipend from the government for her care, as well as social security from Mercedes. Marissa didn't need the money and it gave her a small amount of joy to know she could put that money away in trust for Jenna to have when she started college.

Ruben's estate had been seized by the government and was likely to be tied up in asset recovery for years but if there was anything left it was to go to Jenna as his only living heir. Ruben's mother died of an infection from her broken hip so that left the road free and clear for Jenna, although Marissa had reservations about accepting money that had been banked on the misery of others. It was blood money and someday when Jenna was older, she'd explain this to her and let her make her own choice about the money. She hoped Jenna wouldn't want it but that decision was a long way off from today.

There was a knock at the door and Marissa rose to open it.

"Agent Hawker," she said, surprised to see him at her door, lounging idly at the door frame. "What can I do for you? Is everything all right?"

She was still a little leery of him, remembering how cold and relentless he'd been in that interrogation room when she'd thought he was trying to take her down for kidnapping.

"Archer needs you," he stated bluntly.

She stepped away. "What is this about?"

"This is about a man giving up everything for a woman who kicked him to the curb not once but twice. This is about a woman who has a peculiar way of showing her gratitude to a man who would willingly take a bullet in her place. That's what this is about."

"Well, then I don't see how it's any of your business, Agent Hawker. Good day," she said, attempting to close the door but he stopped it with the flat of his hand, making her jump.

"Not yet," he warned and she took a step back,

alarmed. "I'm here to say my piece and you're going to listen."

"I've heard enough," she said, her heart fluttering hard in her chest. She didn't want to hear how Archer was suffering. It would only serve to make her feel worse for being unable to be there for him.

"You haven't heard the half of it. Archer quit the branch a month ago. He's gone."

Archer quit the branch? "Why?" she whispered, looking to Jeremiah for answers. "Why would he do that? He loves the job."

"He used to love the job. Now he loves something—or someone—else more. Yet, here you are. And you're both alone."

Marissa jerked. "He shot Ruben in cold blood," she stated. "The man I knew would never do that."

"The man I know couldn't let a murderer get away with what he'd done to two women, one of whom he'd die for. Do you know he sat by your bedside night and day while you were in a coma? That he didn't even leave to shower or eat. Whatever food he managed to shove down his throat, we brought to him."

She knew this. But how was she supposed to reconcile herself to the fact that the man she loved was capable of such an atrocity? She understood that in the course of his job he'd had to use deadly force to protect himself or others in the past and she didn't fault him for it but what had happened with

Ruben...she'd seen it in his eyes that it had been nothing like that. She blinked back tears. "He should've let the law run its course," she maintained stubbornly, and if she were being honest, cowardly.

"You're right. And if he had, Ruben would likely be out on a technicality and you'd be constantly looking over your shoulder, waiting and wondering when he was coming for you. He said as much to Archer that day. Promised it, in fact. Make no mistake, Marissa...that man planned to do far worse to you than what you endured that night at the compound. Archer couldn't live with that. Wouldn't allow it. He did what was necessary. And if no one else is judging him, why are you?"

Her mouth worked but no sound came out. Finally, she managed to whisper, "Why'd he have to do it?"

Jeremiah looked grim as he answered. "He did it because he felt he didn't have a choice. Given the options...I can't say you wouldn't have done the same."

"I wouldn't kill a man," she countered.

"You already have," he reminded her. "To save Jenna." He turned to leave but added, "Careful of that blood on your own hands, you never know what you'll end up staining when you try to wipe it away."

CHAPTER TWENTY

IT WAS A LONG TIME before the tears stopped coming after Agent Hawker left. She wanted to scream at him for awakening her desperate need to forgive Archer for whatever he'd had to do to keep them safe but it was there and suddenly loud in its despair.

She tucked herself into a ball and rocked, closing her eyes to everything but the ardent wish that life hadn't been so cruel to the people she cared about.

She thought of Mercedes, her beloved, bigger-than-life sister who had brought her wild and crazy energy to everything she'd ever set her heart on doing and how when she left this world she'd done it in a big way. Marissa thought with a tear-soaked smile how Mercedes would've laughed off Marissa's moral dilemma with a shrug and a flip "he deserved it" before moving on.

She thought of Layla, who'd done nothing to earn her fate except be her friend and coworker. She remembered how Layla used to love pickle and mayonnaise sandwiches yet declared beanie-weenies inedible. She choked on the rising bubble of hysterical laughter and wished Layla were here to try and convince her that if everyone turned vegetarian the world would be a better place.

Layla's voice faded and Marissa wiped away her tears.

But if Layla and Mercedes were here they'd call her crazy for pushing away a good man. Her cheeks burned as she recalled Jeremiah's parting statement. Yes, she had killed a man to protect Jenna and she'd do it again if need be.

So, Archer had done what needed to be done to keep them safe. How was that wrong? In the eyes of the law it was wrong, she answered, but it was weak at best and quickly losing ground.

When Ruben was beating her within an inch of her life, she'd hoped Archer would riddle him with bullets and that he'd suffer a thousand torments as he slowly bled out. Yet, she'd blacked out thinking she was going to die hanging from the ceiling and Ruben was going to do awful things to Jenna. At that moment, she would've given her soul to keep that from happening.

Perhaps it had been no different for Archer. She couldn't imagine the guilt he carried, or the image of her he had stuck in his mind during her worst hour.

Shame burned, hot and deep, and she buried her head against her knees until Jenna toddled over to her and leaned her little head against her in some attempt to offer comfort. Marissa lifted her head and offered a smile but it hurt even to do that. "Oh, *mija,* I've made a terrible mistake. What should I do now?"

Jenna grinned and sucked on her finger, her world none the worse for wear for their tragedy and Marissa had Archer to thank for that. Marissa smoothed a curl away from Jenna's sweet face and sighed unhappily.

Jenna frowned and plopped down on her diapered behind and Marissa hiccupped softly. "That's how I feel, too," she acknowledged, tears brimming in her eyes. "I just don't know how to fix everything that went wrong."

ARCHER DIDN'T KNOW WHAT the hell he was doing. He'd spent the past few weeks trying to convince himself that turning in his badge had been the right decision but then the empty house had mocked him at every turn and he wondered if he was about to lose his mind.

And then it became clear—blindingly so. It wasn't the house or the job that was driving him crazy. It was that he'd left without a fight.

He'd tucked his tail under his legs and ran at the first sign that Marissa was rejecting him again. He'd seen it in her eyes that she was hurt and confused, but instead of sitting down with her and holding her until she saw clearly again, he'd bolted.

Just like the last time. He hadn't fought. He'd

given up. Walked away in an angry sulk, pissed-off at the world because he'd been too much of a coward to fight for what was important.

Not this time. If she wanted to kick him out of her life she'd have to put her back into it because he wasn't ready to walk away without putting it all out there.

He went to her apartment but she wasn't there. He checked his watch. Not quite five o'clock. So he detoured to her work. He was just bounding up the stairs going toward the double glass doors when he saw her coming out of a side building, carrying Jenna.

He stopped and their stares locked. He didn't waste time and strode toward her.

"I've come to tell you something," he stated before she could open her mouth and before he could lose his nerve. "I love you. I killed a man and I'd do it again if it meant keeping the people I love safe. I'm not perfect. I'm hotheaded, mean-tempered when I haven't had my coffee, and I've even been accused of being a sore loser, but one thing I'm not is a coward. That's why I'm here. I'm not going to keep running from the way I feel about you. And I'm not going to let you run away from the way you feel about me, either, just because you're going through some kind of latent guilt over a dirtbag sadist who got his kicks by mutilating women. If you need counseling to help get you through this, we'll find the best damn head doc money can buy. Whatever it takes…I'll do it because, Marissa Vasquez, you're my world and without you in it, I'm just going through the motions."

She swallowed but said nothing even as her eyes filled. He expected her to try and push him away again but he held his ground, showing her that he was willing to be her rock if she would only let him. And if that meant she needed someone to shoulder the burden of the past because it was too heavy for her, he was the man to do it.

"I never saw myself as a man who could live a normal life but I've come to realize it wasn't the normal part that scared me. It was the threat of losing it, should I ever be so blessed to have it. My old man taught me that life is short so take your pleasure where you can but I had it all wrong. I was running away from anything that represented stability instead of embracing it. Hell, what I'm trying to say is…I want to embrace a life with you and Jenna. I want you to rearrange my furniture as many times as you like, plant flowers and hang bird feeders if you want. I want to argue over whose turn it is to check the mail at the end of the driveway and watch late-night television with you tucked against my side, falling asleep together halfway before the show is over. I want to go to backyard barbecues and drink beer with my friends and wink at you from across the way as you chat over the potato salad with the wives. I want it all. The good, the bad, the boring. Everything." He took a chance and closed the gap between them. He touched her stomach reverently and said softly, "But most of all I want Jenna to have plenty of brothers and sisters to play with and I want to hear our home filled with their laughter."

Marissa's eyes welled and tears spilled down her cheeks but he didn't sense sadness and that gave him hope. "Tell me I made the right choice to fight and not walk away this time," he said, choking on his own words.

She jerked in an uneven nod as she pulled him to her, sealing her mouth to his. He feasted on her lips and tasted her tears. She slid her mouth across his in the sweetest kiss that spoke of gratitude, heartbreak, longing and desire but mostly of love, and Archer knew he'd made the right choice.

"Thank you for not giving up," she whispered against his neck, clinging to him as if he might disappear if she opened her eyes. "Please...take us home. I'm ready, too. For everything."

EPILOGUE

MARISSA CHATTED WITH Tasha Halvorsen and caught Archer's lusty stare from across the yard, laughing when Josh teased him about it.

"I've never seen Archer so happy," Tasha remarked. "I'm guessing he's not missing the old day job."

She laughed and rubbed her distended belly. "I've kept him too busy," she admitted, blushing only a little at the innuendo. Newlyweds were supposed to be constantly eager to touch. But even if they hadn't just celebrated their first anniversary, Marissa knew it would be the same. They both shared an appetite for one another that was equal in proportion to the other.

"How about you? Do you miss your job back at the lab?" Tasha asked.

Marissa thought about it and aside from a pang of nostalgia, she didn't miss it at all. Back in the city she'd been driven to be better than where she came from but she was no longer haunted by that sense of inadequacy. Her nest egg was safe and secure and they lived quite nicely on Archer's pension and savings he banked from his years with the service and the branch. Eventually, they would both look for jobs but for now, they were just making up for lost time and savoring every minute until they were bleary-eyed with fatigue from the new baby.

"I've heard you're having another girl," Tasha commented, patting Marissa's belly softly. "Have you decided on a name?"

At that Marissa quieted. From the moment they discovered they were having a girl, they'd known what her name was going to be. It had seemed the perfect choice.

"Her name is Layla Mercedes," she answered softly, hoping her friend and sister would be happy with the choice and that they were smiling down on them. "And if she turns out to love pickle and mayonnaise sandwiches and have a penchant for drama I'll know for sure it was the right name for her."

Tasha chuckled with a quizzical expression but Marissa didn't elaborate. She wandered over to Archer and leaned into him, smiling as he watched Jenna play with the Halvorsen kids running around.

"Have I told you how much I love you?" she murmured.

"Not today," he said with a somber expression that was as fake as a two-dollar bill.

"Well, let me rectify that." She lifted on her tiptoes

and rubbed her nose against his. "I am crazy in love with you, Archer Brant. What do you think about that?"

He grinned like a man who had the world on a platter and wrapped his arms around her body, loving the feel of her rounded bump against him, and said, "I think that makes me the luckiest man alive." Then he leaned down to tickle her ear with a whisper. "What say we cut out early…"

"I thought you couldn't wait for a piece of Tasha's apple pie?" she said coyly.

"What if I told you, you were the only thing that would satisfy my raging sweet tooth?"

She grinned up at him, full to bursting with all the love and fulfillment a woman had a right to have and offered in a husky tone, "Then I'd say I'll go get my purse while you offer our goodbyes."

He growled and lightly pinched her behind as she hurried away. "I love a woman of action."

She laughed. Life was good.

* * * * *

*Harlequin Intrigue top author Delores Fossen
presents
a brand-new series of
breathtaking romantic suspense!*
TEXAS MATERNITY: HOSTAGES
The first installment available May 2010:
THE BABY'S GUARDIAN

Shaw cursed and hooked his arm around Sabrina.

Despite the urgency that the deadly gunfire created, he tried to be careful with her, and he took the brunt of the fall when he pulled her to the ground. His shoulder hit hard, but he held on tight to his gun so that it wouldn't be jarred from his hand.

Shaw didn't stop there. He crawled over Sabrina, sheltering her pregnant belly with his body, and he came up ready to return fire.

This was obviously a situation he'd wanted to avoid at all cost. He didn't want his baby in the middle of a fight with these armed fugitives, but when they fired that shot, they'd left him no choice. Now, the trick was to get Sabrina safely out of there.

"Get down," someone on the SWAT team yelled from the roof of the adjacent building.

Shaw did. He dropped lower, covering Sabrina as best he could.

There was another shot, but this one came from a rifleman on the SWAT team. Shaw didn't look up, but he heard the sound of glass being blown apart.

The shots continued, all coming from his men, which meant it might be time to try to get Sabrina to better cover. Shaw glanced at the front of the building.

So that Sabrina's pregnant belly wouldn't be smashed against the ground, Shaw eased off her and moved her to a sitting position so that her back was against the brick wall. They were close. Too close. And face-to-face.

He found himself staring right into those sea-green eyes.

How will Shaw get Sabrina out?
Follow the daring rescue and the heartbreaking
aftermath in THE BABY'S GUARDIAN
by Delores Fossen,
available May 2010 from Harlequin Intrigue.

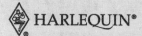

HARLEQUIN®

American ★ Romance®

LAURA MARIE ALTOM

The Baby Twins

Stephanie Olmstead has her hands full raising her twin baby girls on her own. When she runs into old friend Brady Flynn, she's shocked to find herself suddenly attracted to the handsome airline pilot! Will this flyboy be the perfect daddy— or will he crash and burn?

Babies
&
Bachelors
USA

"LOVE, HOME & HAPPINESS"

www.eHarlequin.com

HAR75309

REQUEST YOUR FREE BOOKS!

2 FREE NOVELS PLUS 2 FREE GIFTS!

HARLEQUIN®

Super Romance®

Exciting, emotional, unexpected!

HSR10R

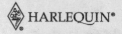

HARLEQUIN®

Showcase

On sale May 11, 2010

Reader favorites from the most talented voices in romance

Save $1.00 on the purchase of 1 or more Harlequin® Showcase books.

HARLEQUIN®

Super Romance®

COMING NEXT MONTH

Available May 11, 2010

#1632 TEXAS TROUBLE
Home on the Ranch
Kathleen O'Brien

#1633 UNTIL HE MET RACHEL
Spotlight on Sentinel Pass
Debra Salonen

#1634 DO YOU TAKE THIS COP?
Count on a Cop
Beth Andrews

#1635 HER HUSBAND'S PARTNER
More than Friends
Jeanie London

#1636 AN HONORABLE MAN
Return to Indigo Springs
Darlene Gardner

#1637 LOVE POTION #2
Margot Early